NO LAND
OF MINE

No Land of Mine

Daniel Pfaff

Published by Grapevine Publishing
Grapevine Publishing, S6533 Hill Point Road
Hill Point, Wisconsin 53937, U.S.A.

First American Edition
Published in 2022 by Grapevine Publishing

ISBN 9798218098933

CHAPTER
One

⤎⤏

ENDANGERED

David Willis stood in the forest and folded a faded, wrinkled paper map. He'd found the map squashed and crumpled in the bottom of a lime green filing cabinet in the ecology department down the hall from his small office where he worked. At some point, one of the corners had been ripped. The tape used to fix it had turned brownish-yellow and brittle. The initials K.G. were penciled onto the lower left-hand corner. If David's research was accurate, the map had belonged to a land conservationist from the 1960s who knew the location of rare orchids throughout the state that many people now believed to be extinct.

He replayed in his mind the strong but valid arguments he'd heard from citizens against a mining company destroying pristine land in the area. He'd listened to their complaints and worries early that morning and told them they needed to band together and demand transparency from the company and from elected officials. But the suggestion only angered them, as he named politicians they'd voted for and supported who'd had a hand in pushing the mine through. Because the power of his position at the state was limited, with this map in his hand, maybe there was a possibility the EPA would help. Perhaps they'd also be able to save him from the abuse and heat he was taking for holding out and doing his job ensuring the laws were being followed.

When he approached a clearing thirty feet ahead of him, he saw the outline of a dainty-looking plant. It didn't fit the rest of the horticulture consisting of cedars, ferns, and snakeroot plants. He stooped low to the ground as he raised his camera. A blurry, colorful image came into focus through the lens he held beneath the canopy of plants, giving him a better look. He held his finger on the button, which was in rapid succession mode, then lowered the Canon EOS R7.

When he moved within five feet of the strange-looking speci-men, which proudly displayed a uniquely purple flower, he stood motionless as someone would when meeting extraterrestrial life. He identified the species as *Calypso bulbosa*. He knew then what he figured the mining company knew all along—there were more likely others. He suspected the apathetic statements about the plant being extinct were to get him to sign off on a conditional land use permit.

He moved in for a closer examination while slinging the camera to his back. He used his hands to part the ferns until both knees rested on the soil.

"*Calypso bulbosa*," he said. "The fairy slipper."

The delicate purple flower wavered in the breeze. David gently brushed the petals with the back of his hand, stood again, and took a picture with his iPhone. He'd only seen the orchids online and in textbooks, but there was no mistaking the exqui-site flower's purple and white colors, feather-like petals, and egg shape. He remembered a lecture his botany professor gave about the increasing rarity of the plant. Climate change was impacting its ability to survive.

He put his iPhone in his pocket and the map in his backpack. He snapped a couple of photos with the camera before lowering it. Then he reached for his collapsible army shovel strapped to his backpack. He doubted the discovery of one rare orchid would be enough to stand against the political forces controlled by the mining company. He wanted to take the orchid home to transplant it to save it, even if it was illegal to disturb it. But he knew the odds of the ancient flower surviving after the roots had been disturbed were slim. The plant wouldn't survive the long trek back to the vehicle. Even if by some miracle it did, the plant would never adjust to soil and temperature conditions beyond where it had been growing naturally for thousands of years. David's grip on the handle loosened. The shovel slid back into place. He took a drink of rum and Coke from a flask.

He removed his phone again, opened an app, and marked the location. In case the app didn't record it, he pulled out the conservation map again and made a mental note of the flower's proximity to the X the old land conservationist with the initials K.G. had made years ago on the paper.

When David tried using his cellphone to send a photo of the orchid, the message in the upper left-hand corner read, *No Service*.

A branch in the distance snapped, causing him to startle. He crouched among the ferns. At first he thought it was a deer, or maybe even a black bear, as he was miles away from the crowds of people at the nearby state park at Clearview Lake. When he saw it was Aaron, a guy who worked for the mining company, fumbling toward him through the forest, he realized the mistake he had made telling his supervisor where he was going and what he was looking for.

As Aaron came into the clearing, David noticed he was carrying a rifle.

David unzipped his backpack and took out a can of pepper spray. He slowly backed away from the flower.

"Idiots," he whispered. "This is what I get for doing the right thing. And now they're a threat to all of us."

He wished he'd told his fiancé everything, but because he loved her, he had avoided any talk of work whenever they were together.

CHAPTER
Two

THE INTERVIEW

FBI agent Miranda Fetting sat at a booth inside the chateau at Clearview Lake State Park. She was casually looking at flights to Aruba on her laptop. The cheapest she could find was only one way. But maybe a one-way ticket and getting trapped on a tropical island wouldn't be so terrible, she thought. If she couldn't afford a ticket home, she could probably find some detective work in the tropics. There had to be tourists who were always misplacing belongings, like luggage, or even husbands or wives. She considered how helping travelers would be much less mentally and physically strenuous than what she was currently doing—solving the worst homicide cases and finding clues and truths others didn't want her to discover. She clicked on her bank account balance and sighed heavily—only $236.

"Aruba," she said. "Note to self: start saving."

She was thirty-two but felt older because of the scars left on her body from knife and bullet wounds.

She checked her watch and looked from the open dining area filled with booths, where she sat toward the entrance, one hundred feet away from where people were gathered. She was witnessing people's reactions to a crime scene as news and rumors spread about what had happened yesterday afternoon. Campers who planned to stay the week at the state park stood in groups cupping their early morning mugs of steaming hot chocolate or coffee.

Some women were wrapped in towels or blankets because of the cold, and the husbands, boyfriends, and girlfriends stood behind them in clusters rubbing their shoulders or hugging them. Their behavior was abnormal for a state park in such a pristine location on a late spring morning, and their mood added to the feeling of despondence.

Miranda sat alone at her table far away from the crowd. She looked like a tourist who hadn't yet heard the news. She quietly clicked on images of Aruba's beaches, each photo making it appear that the white beach sand went for miles, and the water seemed clear enough to see down two hundred feet.

She lost track of time as she clicked on images of palm trees. She found a picture of the ocean-side pool at the Ritz-Carlton.

"You must be Special Agent Fetting?" said a male voice that interrupted her concentration.

Miranda redirected her eyes from the computer screen to a man wearing a badge and a dark blue raincoat standing over her. His eyes were hazel, and there was stubble on his chin. With just a slight gray in his brown hair, she guessed him to be in his early forties. And then her eyes drifted downward before looking up again. She'd noticed his uniform pants fit nicely.

"I'm Miranda Fetting."

"Jack Calaway," the man said. He reached to shake her hand. "We spoke on the phone yesterday. I'm the lead detective for the Township of Clearwater."

They released their grip and then flashed their IDs.

Jack slid into the red, cushy booth across the table from her as he put his badge away. He had spoken to her on the phone and had expected to meet an agent who was older and more experienced. Miranda was attractive with blue-green eyes, brown hair, and a toned body.

Jack recognized she wasn't wearing FBI markings. This was the first time he knew of an FBI field agent ever coming to Clearwater. Maybe it wasn't unusual that she wasn't wearing the government-issued cap and jacket. She was fashionable and younger than he was. He concluded maybe the new generation of federal investigators had a different way of dressing. He had nothing on which to gauge her choice to wear designer clothing other than what he'd seen on TV.

"So a biologist was found within the boundaries of the state park," said Miranda. "Apparently, word has already spread to the vacationers that the death wasn't accidental."

Jack unzipped his coat, took it off, and folded it neatly on the seat beside him. "A young couple came across the body when they were out for a hike, but they've been with the police all morning. Someone else must have leaked that it was a murder. The victim is David Willis," he said.

Miranda spun the laptop screen around without acknowledging the name or Jack's description of details surrounding the discovery of the body. Jack could see the blue water and the powdery white sand in the pixelated photos on the screen.

The images of the island paradise made Jack question whether Miranda had even heard him explain how the body had been found. He didn't ask her if she needed the information repeated because he found himself staring at her. Jack looked again at her face and the freckles that lightly dotted her nose. He thought, at most, she might be thirty. Considering she had to have some college degree to work for the FBI, he calculated that she couldn't have worked the job for more than five or six years. He considered her lack of focus might be because she'd been traumatized by what she'd seen in the last case she'd worked and was transitioning into this one—either that or she was already conditioned to working homicide, and she thought nothing of murder.

"Beautiful ocean views, and I've never been to the tropics," said Jack while looking at the photos she had turned toward him. "Some day, I'll plan a vacation there to see what I'm missing. But what does that picture have to do with this case?"

"It has nothing to do with it, which is the entire point of looking. It's in contrast to what's happening here in this community. Clearwater is sitting on a mountain of copper, making money the number one motive for a murder like this. I'm considering changing careers and leaving the area for someplace safe, like Aruba. There's nothing there to fight over but a spot on the beach to put my towel on," said Miranda. She closed her laptop.

"If island paradise is where you'd rather be," said Jack, "then why aren't you there?"

"Because I don't believe running away from problems solves anything, but mainly because I don't have the money. If I'd been smart and started saving earlier, I'd have something to fall back on when things got rough, like now."

Jack lifted off his ball cap and placed it on the table.

"You have a mining company wanting to purchase land a few miles north of here," Miranda continued.

"I'm aware."

"I doubt the timing of their arrival and the death of this biologist are a coincidence."

"I'm hoping you're wrong, but they could be related. David was doing some sort of reconnaissance work in the area," Jack said. "He was in charge of issuing conditional land use permits for the state. His fiancé didn't know why he was in the state park. Because of the inscription on the forehead, maybe someone was confused and thought he worked for the mining company. One of the radicals protesting the mine might have killed him."

"You don't believe this is a simple hate crime. If you did, you wouldn't have called for assistance," said Miranda. "We'll have to do our own thinking. We have to do better than believing what others tell us happened."

Jack stared at her. He was perplexed that someone so seemingly young with more authority than him wanted to hear *his* opinion about a serious subject.

"You really want to know what I have to say about this?"

"Why would you think otherwise?"

"Because my view of what occurs in this town isn't always

popular. But, as it seems you're willing to listen, my gut reaction is like yours—I think it has something to do with this mining company, which oddly has the support of a lot of people in this area," said Jack.

"If they support it, they're not as informed as they should be, or there could be other reasons like propaganda altering their judgement. Did you get a pathology report?"

"A moment ago in a text. He died sometime late yesterday afternoon. I thought he could have been dumped, so I called the state and questioned where he was supposed to have been working. But no one is returning my call."

"It's probably because David Willis was right where they expected him to be. They're probably the ones who sent him there. And if no one in a busy park heard a gunshot, even if he was killed at the far boundaries, it probably means a silencer was used. I guarantee it was a hit, probably by this mining company, and I know you feel that way too. But something is holding you back from saying so."

Jack collapsed the bill of his cap, reshaped it, and placed it on his head. She'd called him out on his reluctance to declare the murder premeditated, although he believed that's exactly what it was. But to what degree? Could the mining company really be so misguided? And what had she meant by suggesting people at the state level weren't calling him because they were possibly involved? As he sat wrestling with the answer, he didn't hear the compliment she had given him about his belief that the murder was a hit. But if people at the state level were somehow involved or had privileged information about the murder, it added a level of severity to the case he wasn't prepared to handle.

"The fact that no one heard the shot and that no one dumped the body tells us it was planned," said Miranda.

"David Willis had *Save the Forrest* knifed into his forehead. The killer spelled forest with two Rs. If it was a hit and not a simple hate crime, why would someone take the time to scribe something into his forehead?"

"Because violence and desecration coincide with the extent of these people's creativity," said Miranda. "As soon as I was called in for this job, I did some research to see if anything out of the ordinary was happening in this area. And that's when this Global Econ Mining company popped up on the computer. Do you know who they are?"

"Only what we already discussed."

"They've been raiding resources of third-world countries and leaving them in ruins. That's why I think this is more than a hate crime, Jack Calaway. We should be looking at joining other national security organizations that would actually allow us to do something about this type of crime."

Jack could see no signs in her eyes that she was joking with him. Her apprehension over the case and the speed at which she was expressing it, along with comments about joining other law enforcement divisions, was alarming to Jack, although he did like that she'd begun calling him by his first name.

"Let's focus on fleeing to Aruba after we're finished with this," said Jack. "We're two perfectly capable detectives, so I think we should be talking about David Willis. One of the few things we found on him was a flask of rum."

"With the way our power has been restricted by federal bureaucracy and partisan nepotism in recent years, I'll be drinking, too, once we get deep into this."

Miranda studied his eyes for a moment as she waited for him to speak.

Jack tried forming a sentence asking about what she'd meant about the limitations of law enforcement. He experienced levels of bureaucracy and nepotism within his own department. He was counting on federal organizations to be different, which is part of the reason he called her.

"Do you have family in the area?" Miranda asked.

"Yes. I have a son."

"Not a wife?"

"We're divorced. Why do you ask?"

"With the controversy surrounding this company, if we're not getting on a plane and leaving, we should think about what we should do with your son. The people who killed David Willis aren't going to like us investigating them."

"If they took a man's life, then they should be worried about us coming after them."

"How old is your son?"

"He's seventeen."

"David Willis was in his mid-twenties, but I'm sure your son will be perfectly fine if you don't take precautions and protect him."

"We're law enforcement. I doubt someone is bold enough to threaten our families or us in this town," said Jack. "That might happen in the cities, but that doesn't happen out here."

Miranda stared quietly at Jack, questioning if he was being facetious or if he really thought the isolated location of Clearwater deterred criminals from coming after families of law enforcement officers.

"I understand some people have a hang-up about my experience and about taking my advice because of my age and because I'm a woman," said Miranda. "And it's difficult to imagine anything like this can happen to an area like Clearwater, but we're living in a new age of wealth and organized crime. Even after seeing David Willis's body, you still apparently aren't aware of what they're capable of."

"Maybe it's a difference in our age, but I think our badges stand for something when it comes to protecting ourselves and our families."

Jack waited for her to blink as he pulled a plastic Ice Breakers container from his raincoat. He popped open the container to offer her a mint. He tried remembering the last time he'd felt this uncomfortable, and his mind went back a few years to when he lived with his wife. He recalled the name-calling and the fighting and the threats. He didn't know what he'd ever done to deserve the abuse. But in this situation, a woman was cautioning him about his and his son's safety, whereas he was certain his ex-wife wouldn't care what happened to him. He wasn't expecting such concern to be directed toward him.

"You seem like an agent who's seen more than anyone should, and I'm sorry if that's made you anxious," said Jack. "But I think we should do some actual investigating before we jump to conclusions and start making assumptions about what this really is. Let's not overreact and think this is a worst-case scenario."

"I think I'm being extremely calm, knowing I'll need to bring a county detective up to speed on this one."

Jack leaned forward and wanted to place his hand on her arm to regain her focus and trust. He didn't like how they seemed to have gone down a different path.

"I don't want to traumatize my family by telling them to be afraid if there's no need for them to worry," said Jack. "If this turns out to be nothing after I told them it was something, I stand to lose credibility with my son. And I don't want to risk damaging my relationship with him, because it's already fragile."

Miranda thought Jack's admission was a naive way to confess he wasn't fully prepared for what they might find during this investigation. But in Jack's defense, grasping the seriousness of the case within only minutes, as she explained it, would be difficult for many county detectives, having lived their entire lives in the Northwoods of the Midwest. Neglecting her advice about ensuring his son's safety seemed ill-advised, but she had no investment in him other than knowing she would need his help. She questioned why she even cared about persuading him to take care of his family in the first place.

As a symbol of peace, she picked up a mint from the container and popped it into her mouth.

"Ideally, the way this works is our departments are supposed to complement each other and not see the job as something to pass off to each other. I only mention it because lately, government agencies that used to work in unison are intentionally becoming fractured by a shift in policy," said Miranda. "Even though I'm younger and a woman, I'll need you to pay attention to everything I tell you, even if you choose not to act on it."

"This is beyond the scope of what my department can handle. I'm not ashamed to admit that, and I don't think of myself as sexist, so I'll try to do whatever you ask as long as it doesn't involve family."

"Then those are terms that will have to do for the moment. The rest of the issues will have to work themselves out as we go."

Miranda sat up straight in her seat and calmly reopened the laptop. She clicked on an open tab to the right of the one that showed the blue ocean off the coast of Aruba. She spun the screen around to show Jack a newspaper article from *The Milwaukee Gazette.*

"So we can better understand the task in front of us," Miranda said, "here's what I think is happening. 'Global Econ Mining Sets Sights on Wisconsin,'" she said, reading the article's title. "It's probably like you said—this company most likely needed David Willis to sign off on some permit granting them access, and he wouldn't comply. But so you understand the damage these people inflict, the company is being sued by a South American country for destroying a river near a fishing village. The people relied on it for their livelihood. Rumors of dead bodies of those who resisted have been surfacing, that sort of thing. And with that in mind, I wouldn't doubt if more turn up in this area. It seems they've been embedded here long before the media announced their arrival."

"Why would you think that?"

"Tell me about *The Clearwater Chronicle*," said Miranda.

"They're local. I drove there around four-thirty last night and issued them a statement about a body being discovered. We use them all the time. They're a small, family-owned paper."

Miranda opened another tab on the computer. "They're already providing detailed information this morning about the victim ahead of the investigation."

"I issued a statement about a body being discovered and asked if anyone had information to come forward. But that was it."

"If you didn't give them any details about the body's condition, someone is probably paying them to create a red herring. We already have our lead," said Miranda. "This newspaper is reporting that hikers found a mutilated body, and it goes so far as to say environmental terrorists are the suspects."

"I told them about the hikers, but I never said anything about an environmentalist being a suspect or the body being mutilated."

"Then we know the extent of this murder. The people of Clearwater, at least those at *The Chronicle*, are wrapped up in this. And that suggests there's already a network, maybe even globally."

"We should talk to them before accusing them of anything."

Jack leaned forward to see the screen. He read the article in its entirety. Then he pushed the computer toward Miranda and leaned back in his seat. Miranda had snuck a peek of the blue lake through the paned window while he was reading, but she turned away from the tranquil view when Jack slid the computer back to her.

"They must have misunderstood me. That's not the story I gave them," said Jack. "I only wanted to head off rumors and inform the public why there's gonna be so much police traffic in the state park. Jeff must have been mistaken."

"Someone claimed the suspect was an environmentalist and a terrorist, and whoever published the press release stated that the report came from the police. That's deception if I've ever seen it. That's not a mistake."

"They must have had a lapse in judgment," said Jack.

Miranda brushed her bangs away from her eyes. Jack thought she looked too pretty to be an FBI agent. He could see she was trying to be patient with him, but no matter how beautiful and sharp she seemed, he wasn't about to declare people he knew at the newspaper guilty of covering up a murder—not without talking with them first. He'd known them for years.

"If we talk with them," said Miranda, "we'll get a read on where the story came from. We might even get a name, and then we'll know the extent of the trouble we're in."

Miranda expected him to say something more, but Jack remained silent. She'd seen from the light in his eyes that he was curious about her. She didn't dislike that he was looking, but she didn't know if he'd turn out to be like the others who fixated on her looks instead of the job. This time she needed a qualified detective to help her solve this murder case. She wondered if Jack could handle whatever obstacles they were confronted with.

She twisted the ends of her hair as she turned again to look out at the lake. She'd been pulled off a case in the Twin Cit-ies during the night. It was a homicide that she'd practically wrapped up that she'd had to hand off. She was tired of doing all of the legwork for other detectives, who then benefited from her hard work.

For now, Miranda had to let go of how unfairly her supervi-sor had treated her by moving her from place to place, doing the bulk of the work. She wrote on the table with her finger. *I should have been a writer, something more artistic.*

"I know you probably expected an entire fleet of agents to arrive, but we're short-handed at the moment, so I want you to stay close to me," said Miranda.

"I would expect to stay in close contact and share whatever we find."

"Usually, I check out the body and the crime scene, but I don't think it's necessary this time. Do you already have a foren-sics team at work on it?"

"Bill Winslow, our forensic investigator, is on it."

"Is he trustworthy? Or do you think he's someone who could be easily bribed?"

"He works for the department, so he's trustworthy, and, of course, he's not going to accept bribes," said Jack, expecting a response.

Miranda ignored him. It wasn't clear to Jack if she'd even heard him. It was as though she was going over a checklist or shopping list in her mind.

"One more thing we need to consider is that David Wil-lis was within the boundaries of the state park. I bet he knew the mining company was probably scoping it out to take it. He probably tried to block it from happening somehow. That would explain why he was killed there. I bet he was looking for some-thing."

Jack's face remained expressionless. He momentarily consid-ered the possibility that this woman was crazy to think that plans to steal the state park in secret were occurring. But Miranda, having brought up concerns about the state for the second time, sat with a straight face. The blue in her eyes reminded him of the ocean she'd alluded to earlier. As conspiracy-minded as Miranda appeared to Jack, she didn't seem to him to be the type who would lie. But her accusation about the state park that included miles of virgin land sounded too absurd.

"A mining company can't simply take a state park because they want it," said Jack. "I think we might be reaching."

"I hope we're wrong, but I don't put anything beyond the reach of these people. The kind of money they flaunt is rarely earned by relying on only moral principles."

From Jack's tired and distanced look, Miranda sensed the information was jarring him.

"Did you find any electronics on the body—a camera, a phone?" she asked. She felt it was necessary to redirect the conversation toward something more tangible.

"David's fiancé said he would have had his phone, so whoever killed him must have taken it," said Jack. "Forensics is still at the scene, so if Bill finds anything more, he'll call or text when he has reception. And we put a trace on David's phone, but so far, we've gotten nothing."

Jack began thinking about the previous comment she'd made. Could an entire lake and the surrounding forested ecosystem simply be erased by bulldozers, chainsaws, and excavators? The whole idea was unimaginable. The entire town of Clearwater would vanish if the park did.

"If they weren't on the body, there's no point in even looking for electronics because the people responsible aren't going to have his belongings in their possession," said Miranda. "I'm sure they've already been destroyed. You were right in knowing this wasn't a petty murder theft or a random homicide."

She gave Jack one last good look. Although she sometimes saw his eyes roaming, and even though he seemed naive, Jack had a kind, appealing way about him, unlike many other detectives she'd met who only wanted to hit on her. There was some substance to Jack.

She glanced again at the pictures of Aruba and sighed before closing the laptop.

"This case is going to be one of the most challenging I've

worked on, so I want to be clear that we're going to be working closely together on this," she said.

Jack looked at Miranda impatiently. "I am with you. I already told you I am. It's my job."

"You don't understand. I want you to work with me directly like you're my partner—traveling together, eating together."

"I don't spend that much time with anyone."

"You'll need to start changing your habits. We both will because we will probably need each other to get through this. This is one of the first cases of its kind to hit the Midwest, and with recent attacks on government, it'll be a test to see how much power you and I still have."

CHAPTER
Three

LEARNING TO SURF

Rita Fetting had been conditioned to work. It was the same for almost everyone else in the Midwestern farming community she was born into. From the time she was little to when she was in her late teens, there were always grueling chores to do. Every day, twice a day, she'd slip on her muddy rubber boots that rubbed the back of her heels raw. Throughout the farm, she had to lug feed for cattle, calves, chickens, goats, and an occasional pig. And then there were the calluses that formed on her fingers. The milking of cows and the slinging of the hatchet while butchering chickens took its toll on her once delicate grip. At Sunday church service, which the family attended regularly, she and her older sister, Linda, were repeatedly told their lifestyle consisted of hard but honest work. The preacher, standing in clean white cloth, told them anyone not working with their hands for a living was doing easier, more dishonest work. No one questioned the remark's validity because the saying reinforced what they were doing in their own lives and that it was right.

But it was always Linda who never questioned, who always accepted what they were told. It was the opposite for Rita. When Rita wasn't helping slaughter animals for meat, cooking, canning, feeding cattle, or occupying her time satisfying her family's expectations, she'd lock the door to her room and read. She loved the classics—*Pride and Prejudice*, *To Kill a Mockingbird*, *Charlotte's Web*, *The Count of Monte Cristo*, and *Dracula*. Those times alone with her books as a teenager were the favorite of her day, but they never lasted. Duty always pulled her away from her escape of reading. She often had to entertain and impress a family member or neighbor with her piano playing because her parents demanded it. She noticed how their faces glowed as though they were the ones playing the difficult melodies. But it was all bearable as long as her sister, Linda, was around to share the hardships they were born into. When Linda married and left the family farm to raise a family of her own and to repeat the same cycle she'd been born into, Rita understood she didn't want to do the same.

With her high school diploma, a packed suitcase, and small savings in her purse, Rita jumped on a Greyhound and took it to where she heard no one would judge her for taking a risk. California had a liberating feel to it. Rita had only been there for six years but was doing well for herself. She'd made friends by joining an online group, one of the first on the internet. And she was surprised by the amount of help and support she'd received in relocating. The people seemed genuine, not wanting anything in return for their help. They simply wanted her to do well and gain a foothold because they'd taken the same chance. It was an outpouring of guilt-free acceptance she'd never before felt.

She was preparing to have some of her closest friends over for supper, as she did once a month. They would eat and then sit on the patio and drink white wine under paper lanterns while marveling over the colorful stucco-type buildings and the endless ocean. And she loved the ocean for its vast loneliness and beauty, but she loved it more for how it brought people to the water. Near the ocean, the possibilities were endless.

She'd just opened a bottle of chardonnay. She'd thrown the cork in a glass where she kept a collection of them. She was singing along to Roxette when the phone rang. She turned the music down and picked up the cordless receiver. She expected it to be Rachel, the one friend who was never on time. Her lateness was the joke between the two. But the woman on the other end had Rita verify her name. Then she said she was listed as an emergency contact. After being told for whom, she was informed her brother-in-law had been killed in a car accident, and Linda, her sister, had severe head trauma and most likely wouldn't survive. Then, before the call ended, she was told that her sister had died.

The news was sudden, not slow and drawn out, which would have given her time to prepare. When Rita learned her sister and brother-in-law, Mark, hadn't survived, she slumped toward the floor. Before the phone slipped from her fingertips, she remembered hearing, "The little girl, Miranda, was miraculously okay. She didn't have a scratch on her."

Rita called her friend Rachel to tell her the news and explain that dinner was canceled. She had to leave town for a while (for how long, she didn't know), and she asked Rachel to take care of her plants and her pet fish, Wilbur, while she was gone. She also leased and operated a tiny bookstore in Half Moon Bay, so she asked Rachel if she could find someone to fill in for her while she was gone. She hadn't been back to Ohio since she was eighteen. She could never convince her sister and brother-in-law to move where she saw more opportunity to grow and be herself, but now there was nothing to argue about.

Back in Ohio, shortly after the funeral, she had the adoption papers drawn up and made it legal. She moved the little girl, Miranda, to the Golden State.

As a way to help both of them deal with the constant feeling of loss and grief, whenever Miranda needed a break between reading and schoolwork, when the waves were calm, only a year after the ink on the adoption paperwork was dry, Rita tried teaching the little girl with pigtails how to surf. As instructed, Miranda would paddle out onto the ocean. She'd get herself positioned perfectly in front of the rising wave and attempt to leap onto the board and regain her balance. Often she'd lose her footing and tumble headfirst into the cold Pacific water. She'd topple over as though she couldn't hold back the weight of her head and shoulders. The water was so cold Miranda's teeth would click and clatter. Her lips would turn blue. But she'd come up coughing and laughing. Laughing was part of the routine to cope with the fear and the cold. But when the laughing stopped, Rita did her best to answer her niece's questions about her past. She explained that sometimes the best thing to do was to forget the past and start over completely new—to reinvent herself and to be true to herself. If she could do those two things, she'd have a bright future ahead of her.

Miranda was thirteen, and the breeze blowing off the Pacific was gentle when she came to the surf shop as usual with Rita on a Saturday. Instead of surfing that morning, Miranda decided to walk along the shore in search of treasure as she'd often done at sunrise. The beach sand felt like a soft, wet springboard beneath her toes. Noises of gulls filled the air while sandpipers scurried seaward on the wet sand, then landward to the rhythm of the crashing and receding waves. Miranda carried a metal pail and a small scrub brush to collect sea shells. Wearing her favorite pink and tangerine striped one-piece bathing suit, she had just begun collecting shipwrecked sand dollars. She'd inspect and brush off the ones she wanted to keep. Then she'd toss the others into the surf for the rushing water and wet shifting sand to reclaim. At the age of thirteen, she felt the attraction of the ocean, much like her aunt did. It was the same routine every morning, filling her lungs with the ocean breeze and searching the sand for all the treasures the waves had washed ashore from its depths during the night when she slept.

Glancing down the beach, Miranda saw something that hadn't been there the morning before. It was about the size of a baby whale or a seal but didn't look life-like. At first, it looked to her like a treasure chest that had been washed ashore from Singapore or Malaysia. She cast aside her pail of shells and her scrub brush. She took off running. She was fast then and loved pretending she was in a race and that whoever crossed the finish line first got the prize. No one could beat her unless she let them. As she got closer, she slowed to an apprehensive walk. The prize didn't appear to be what it initially seemed. She ruled out a treasure chest filled with stolen pirate gold. She abandoned the thought of running her hands through the shimmering booty.

The object wasn't angular or tall enough to match the pictures of treasure chests she'd seen in the pirate books she'd read at Aunt Rita's bookstore. Nor was she convinced it was some dead animal like a whale or a seal. Those body types didn't fit the profile. A torpedo from a forgotten foreign war now seemed more likely. A torpedo was longer and had a lower, less bulky draft which matched more closely with what she saw. She convinced herself that she'd be surrounded by friends at school wanting to hear that story. That would help the eccentric but bold girl fit in better among her peers. She picked up the pace and ran before slowing down again. The object began moving, rocking back and forth in the surf like a piece of driftwood. As she cautiously continued her approach, she could see the limbs articulate in the waves. They moved like the arms of a jointed puppet.

The object was something other than driftwood or anything else she'd imagined. She took a few steps closer. She could clearly see the body had blonde hair and was an adult male wearing a wetsuit. She moved even closer and noticed his skin was blue. The lenses of his eyes were hazed over like scratched plexiglass that had been rubbed dull by the sand. Miranda turned away at first but couldn't resist the urge to look again. She raced back to the bookshop, where she grabbed a fishing pole.

When her aunt Rita found her, Miranda was sitting in the sand next to the corpse, curiously poking at the body with the fishing rod. Rita rushed over and pulled at her arm.

"Get away from it!" shouted Rita. "We need to leave!"

"Look at the way he rocks in the waves," said Miranda.

"We should go make a phone call," said her aunt. "This isn't anything we can take care of."

"I think someone murdered him, Aunt Rita."

"No, Miranda. He probably went surfing after dark and drowned."

"That's what I thought too, but look."

Before Rita could stop her, Miranda grabbed the body and

rolled it over.

"He has holes in him."

"Leave him, Miranda!"

"We can't just walk away."

"We can't help him!"

"But he belongs to somebody."

"We shouldn't be this close to him!" said her aunt. "You don't even know him."

"He probably left people behind who want to know what happened."

"You have to get over this obsession with trying to fix things that are out of your hands, Miranda. Loss happens. Sometimes bad things just happen."

Her aunt tugged at her, but Miranda defiantly shrugged her hand loose to remain close to the body.

When the police arrived after her aunt had raced off to call them, Miranda was still sitting near the dead surfer.

Rita watched from a distance and paced back and forth until a path was worn in the sand.

The officer stood next to Miranda.

"I couldn't just leave him," said Miranda.

"I remember when I saw my first dead body. I couldn't walk away either," said the officer.

"This isn't my first one," said Miranda.

"What do you mean not your first one?"

"I lost my parents. It was six years ago, and I try to forget it, but I'm not like my aunt."

The police officer knelt in the sand next to the girl.

"Why do people hurt each other?" Miranda asked.

"Some people are just broken and can't heal, and there's no helping them. But you can't let their problems become yours."

"But they are my problems, and now they're yours too. It's not like we live on our own little islands. Our actions matter to everyone around us."

"You're a good detective, but your aunt is right. You shouldn't get caught up in things like this. We should find someone for you to talk to."

"I talk to professionals all the time. I've already met with counselors, who tell me the same thing."

"What do they tell you?"

"They tell me I need to focus on my life and move on, but I tell them to leave me the hell alone and talk to someone else about it. If they want to ignore that there are terrible people in this world who need to be punished for the horrible things they do to others, fine. But they shouldn't let their weak-ass ideals try to scare me away from doing what needs to be done. Someone needs to be brave enough to look at murder. The rest of us need protection so we're safe. And you're a police officer, so you should know that. You go ahead and leave if this guy's death is too difficult to look at, but I'm staying because I'm tired of the adults always wanting to run away from fixing things."

CHAPTER
Four

MISINFORMED

Miranda scrolled through her phone for messages as she and Jack left the chateau at the state park and turned north onto Highway 43. She had still been hoping to hear being assigned to this case had been a mistake or a form of punishment for being critical lately of management in her department. She didn't like how her boss didn't stand up to the newly appointed FBI director, who seemed to favor big business over government oversight. But there were no messages. And no messages meant her boss had placed her in what she saw as a particularly dangerous situation, unassisted, exactly where he wanted her to be. If she wasn't ditching the case and hopping on a plane for Aruba, there was nothing for her to do but lift her chin and grip the steering wheel.

It's too late to undo the choices I've already made, she thought.

She put the phone on the seat between her legs.

Without even thinking, Jack's eyes roamed to where she had placed the phone. He tried looking away before she caught him checking out her body, but his gaze lingered a little too long.

Miranda questioned again how much he'd be able to assist.

"I want to start with this newspaper," Miranda said. "That will be an indicator as to how embedded in your community the people at this mining company are."

"I'm impressed that you seem to have such a good read on this," said Jack. He sat in the passenger seat of the black Camry. He anxiously watched Miranda relying on the blue arrow on the navigation screen to guide them to the hometown newspaper, even though he knew the way just by the turns and feel of the road.

It occurred to Jack that when Miranda had first arrived, she'd already programmed the paper's address into her car's navigation system, even before he had agreed to come along as a stand-in partner.

Miranda must have known he could have provided directions for her just as easily. The fact that Miranda relied on the blue arrow to guide them suggested that she didn't want or didn't yet trust Jack's help. Or maybe she hadn't counted on him coming along with her.

Because of her talk of Aruba and her mention of attacks on the government, he questioned what had happened to her for an FBI agent to exhibit what he thought was overly defensive, guarded behavior. It made him question why she wanted him riding along with her.

"Traveling with you to the newspaper seems like a good start," said Jack, "but spending so much time with you could be an issue."

"For you?"

"For my captain," said Jack. "He was skeptical about me contacting the FBI to begin with."

"He at least had the sense to allow you to call for assistance."

"I don't think Steve had me contact you because he thought we'd be more efficient together. I think he's worried about this case, too, and the attention it could draw to the area. But he was hoping you'd take ownership of it."

"That's not a surprise that he feels that way. But right now, there are bigger things to worry about than jurisdiction. We don't have time to argue over what division does what, not when these people are so organized, Jack. I said we should be a team, and I meant it. If your supervisor has issues with us working together, I'll deal with it when issues arise."

Jack released a deep breath as he tried to relax the muscles at the base of his neck. Miranda's remark that she'd be able to handle his boss relieved some of the stress he was feeling. But he had other concerns. He hoped Miranda would tell him why, if she was already worried about this case because it might involve an international mining company, she hadn't brought along other field agents. If she doubted their ability to solve this case, why not bring in more federal people right now?

Miranda never volunteered an explanation, and Jack was happy, for now, not knowing the answer to his questions simply because she'd asked him to come along. Being asked to ride along with a beautiful FBI agent made him sit taller. It boosted his ego, although riding with her came with other obligations. He knew she was expecting something significant from him beyond the typical county duties he'd become accustomed to. He could already sense it in how she'd asked him to travel with her.

Equally troubling was that when he'd gotten into her car, he noticed that there weren't any license plates on the vehicle. It was black, completely "unmarked." It was another peculiarity adding to Miranda's mystery of not wearing FBI markings. As they traveled farther from his truck, which he'd left at the chateau at the state park, he questioned if Miranda was perceptive enough to sense his concern.

He rubbed the back of his neck, hoping everything mysterious about Miranda would come out when she was ready to tell him. But one question remained of which he wanted more clarification.

"I like the idea of being a team, and I appreciate your advice on how to proceed with this case, and I know I'm relying on you for a lot. But you seem preoccupied. Is everything okay?"

Miranda shot Jack a sideways glance. "I'd like to win the lottery or find a few diamonds on the floor during a raid once in my life that no one claims."

"Back at the park, you talked of wanting to leave for Aruba, but if this case is as problematic as you say, I'm concerned your mind is elsewhere. And I'm not trying to sound mean or critical. I'm only concerned that your focus might not be here with me."

Miranda glanced at herself in the rearview mirror. She wondered if she could tell someone she'd just met, who was depending on her, how the past few cases had made her feel burned out and undervalued.

She knew she was pretty even though she could see in her reflection in the rearview mirror the faint lines beginning to form under her eyes. She was hoping this case wouldn't cause her body more damage. How could she explain to anyone that lately, her concerns centered around herself when they used to center around saving others?

"Aruba will be sure to come up from time to time because it's how I handle my anxiety. But I'll try to stay more on the topic of the case," said Miranda. "The murder of this biologist, or something similar, has been building for a while now because this area needs money. Of course we all need it, but your area has been hit especially hard."

She gripped the steering wheel and took a deep breath.

"The problem with this mining company moving in is that it's an economic one that started forty years ago," she said. "Many people in the Midwest left for coastal areas of the country, my aunt being one of them. The economy in this area suffered. And now there's apparently a group at this particular mining company that knows how to mask itself as these people's savior by promising them the jobs they need for failing to change with the times. Do you want to hear more?"

"Not really, but I know more is coming."

"That's the game we're up against. It's something they do in places like Venezuela. No one in their right mind wants a twenty-mile mine in their backyard, even though it's suggested we need them to help create the technology that will save the planet from climate change. It's messy. I think David Willis was threatening to expose the depth of their operation, and I think their solution was to deal with it by killing him, as we talked about."

Jack turned away from her and looked out the window because it was best to avoid political discussions about the changing economic and environmental climates in his Midwestern community. Families he knew had become divided, arguing about climate change and the loss of their relatives to more prosperous parts of the country.

He felt the urge to reach for the door handle. But then he looked over at Miranda again. She was calm, and there was no yelling. He felt he could listen to the discussion about economics and politics as long as she was the one giving it.

Miranda continued. "Your community is now at the epicenter of the global energy conversation, and most sensible people step aside and steer clear of the controversy. But you and I are about to dive into the middle of it. And I'm questioning if it's worth the fight when people remain silent when no one is willing to help. I'm on the verge of running away and doing my own thing like most sane people would do."

She checked the navigational system again to make sure she remained on course. Then she looked back and forth between Jack's blank expression and the road and waited for him to say something more.

When Jack continued staring ahead, showing no interest in interrupting her, Miranda said, "You can't just take a beautiful area like this. First, you have to convince the people who live here that it's necessary for them to transform the environment they love. I suspect your newspaper, *The Chronicle*, is being paid to be a part of the propaganda machine selling the idea of this mine being the end to everyone's problems. But now they've crossed the line by helping cover up the murder of someone who was lawfully blocking them. It's a corporate war tactic used to disguise an invasion."

Jack didn't want to ask a question because he didn't want to seem completely ignorant. He checked Miranda's face to see if she was serious.

"I'm not trying to be critical, but comparing what's happening here to war seems like a little much," said Jack.

"Maybe. Let's hope I'm wrong, but don't be fooled because bombs aren't falling from planes your area isn't caught up in a war. I'm willing to bet the effort here to hide the truth about why David Willis was murdered is highly organized and militaristic in nature," said Miranda. "I really hope you prove me wrong. That way, we can talk about more interesting things, like world travel and books."

Jack wished he'd been able to come up with something witty or flirty to ease the tension, because that's what he usually did. He hoped they could keep their biases out of the investigation. Still, he felt Miranda's pessimistic viewpoint of Clearwater being taken over by a corporation leading a disinformation campaign against the population was one-sided and unsubstantiated.

But he remained silent as he sat, considering everything she'd said. Part of him was impressed with her breakdown of events leading up to David Willis's death. And she seemed smart even if she did mention sometimes wanting to run away.

"Has your connection to these journalists at this newspaper been strictly business?" Miranda asked.

"Yes. I've given them memos and police reports for fifteen years."

"Have you ever known them to twist your reporting before?"

"No. But I'm not sure they lied about my report or did it intentionally. People make mistakes."

"I wish I could see the world through your eyes. They're journalists, meaning they rarely make mistakes, and reputable and ethical ones don't put their own slant on stories. But these people took your story and spun it, and no matter how you try to rationalize it and make excuses for them, that's lying," said Miranda.

"It could be an honest mistake."

"Why are you so defensive of these people?"

"Because I've known them for years."

"I hope you're right. But the article in the paper was subjective, not objective, and if you remember your English classes from years ago, reporting is supposed to be objective. They shouldn't be naming suspects ahead of an investigation, but because they did probably means they've intentionally taken a side."

Jack attempted to recall lessons from his high school English courses. It took him a moment to recollect the tight sweaters his teacher Ms. Jacobs had worn during the winters before he would have learned the terms *subjective* and *objective*.

"I have a difficult time thinking these people would do anything to hurt anyone," he said.

"You're sweet, Jack. And I'm curious to find out how you got this job. They might not have pulled the trigger, but they are hurting people if they're spreading lies about who did it. And it's not completely their fault. Social media has significantly lowered the standards of media."

Miranda scanned the navigation system again, seeing the building up ahead and to the right.

The newspaper, possibly hurting other people by spreading lies, changed Jack's view of what he otherwise had seen as her unwarranted cynicism. Having gone through a messy divorce, the hurtful things people said to each other also mattered to him.

When they turned into the parking lot, Miranda noticed the yellow steel building with brown wainscoting was beginning to show its age. The colors were fading, and the gutters were drooping in one corner. The hedges hadn't been trimmed in several years, blocking some windows.

Jack caught her examining the building's condition.

"The business wasn't able to switch to online print as quickly as they wanted to, or they didn't see the impact social media would have on print journalism," said Jack.

"Which makes them a perfect target to be paid to spread the propaganda for people who want to cover up a murder and take a state park," said Miranda.

Diane, the receptionist, stood ten feet from the door behind a tall, white marble-topped counter. She was of medium height and wore her reddish-blonde hair in a bun. She wore a flowery patterned short dress that showed off her spray-tanned legs accented by her high heels. She was studying a computer screen.

Miranda and Jack planted themselves at the front of the decorative counter. It was obvious to Diane they were there, yet Jack and Miranda waited to be acknowledged.

After a minute, Miranda checked her watch.

"Excuse us," she announced, having waited another fifteen seconds without a word being spoken. "We're here to talk to the owner or the editor."

Diane, whom Jack had known for years, stood off to the side and continued typing. She never looked up and seemed to purposely busy herself at the keyboard. She was slightly overweight but attractive with soft facial features, and she knew how to project importance in her straight posture.

"Is the editor of the paper here?" Miranda said, this time a little louder.

"I'll answer your questions when I'm ready," said Diane.

She's never too busy to greet anyone, Jack thought. *She always at least checks to see who entered, even if it is only to see if the person is worth talking to.*

"What's your name?" Diane finally asked. Her eyes never left the laptop screen.

"Miranda Fetting."

"I've never heard of the Fettings. Are you local?"

"She's here with me, Diane," said Jack.

Diane startled and then looked up when she recognized Jack's deep voice. It was an odd spectacle for Miranda to witness.

"Jack, don't you have bad guys you should be chasing? Are you just going to stand there checking me out?" teased Diane.

Jack found Miranda extremely attractive and bright, and even though he didn't want to admit it, he sought her approval after spending time in the car talking with her. He didn't want her to think from Diane's behavior that the two were close, because they weren't.

"This is FBI Special Agent Fetting," said Jack. "She's here to assist with this case of the body found in the park."

"Who called in the FBI?" Diane asked.

"I did," said Jack. "But it doesn't matter who called her because she's here to help. We need to talk to Jeff because the statement I gave yesterday isn't accurate. Jeff made some additions to the press release."

"What are you talking about?" Diane asked. She let her arms

dangle at her side as she moved a few steps closer to the counter. The gesture gave both detectives the idea she was genuinely interested in helping. It made them momentarily consider that the paper hadn't done anything intentionally hurtful, like covering up a murder.

"I never gave any specifics about the man's death in the park, but Jeff stated in the paper that it was a murder. He said that an environmentalist was a suspect," Jack explained. "We never discussed any of that."

"We're here to find out if the mining company is paying you to plant a fake story. It's important we talk to your editor to figure out why he falsified a police report to single out innocent people in a death," said Miranda. "It's difficult for us to believe someone would want to do something so vindictive and misleading."

Miranda had taken a step forward, inserting herself into the conversation and leading it where she needed to go. She wanted to be sure Diane knew they weren't simply there for casual conversation.

Miranda wasn't finished. "Personally, I think someone at the mining company who's eyeing this area is paying you to help cover up this death. But you're in the business of being honest and informing people, not lying and trying to mislead them."

Diane's cheeks reddened, and she tilted her head to the side. "Do we need an attorney?" she asked.

"Did you do anything illegal or unethical, like accepting bribes to frame an environmentalist? I certainly hope not. Not someone as kind and caring as yourself."

Diane gulped and folded her arms.

"Jeff Harvey owns the paper, and he's the one you'll have to talk to," she said. "But he hasn't shown up yet unless he came in through the back. Let me check. And Jack, you've got a good-looking boy who's quite an athlete. He doesn't need to see his father being pushed around by out-of-towners, even if they are with the FBI."

Diane disappeared through a door leading to another room.

"You lay it all out there to spark a reaction, don't you," said Jack.

"I'm not buying that small-town charm she's working so hard to sell, although I'd like to. What exactly did you tell them about the murder when you called it in?" Miranda asked.

"I told them hikers found a body and that the circumstances surrounding the death seemed suspicious."

"That was it?"

"Yes. I ran it by Steve."

"And he wouldn't have altered the statement without you knowing?"

"Steve would never contact the paper unless he absolutely had to because he doesn't like the attention. And no one at the department is involved in a cover-up," Jack reassured her.

"Sometimes detectives leak information to impress people they want to hook up with."

"She's not my type," said Jack. "After my divorce, I'm more particular about who I date."

"These are the awkward questions we need to get out of the way right now to make sure no one is covering for someone."

Then Miranda lightly squeezed Jack's hand and let go. Her action caught Jack off guard and puzzled him. *Maybe it was FBI secret code for something*, he thought. *But for what? To stress or apologize for making her point?* He wasn't sure. But then he felt that maybe he was crowding her space or that his comment about being more particular with women following his divorce had made her feel pity toward him, which he didn't want. After she let go, he took a few steps away to give her more room. But then, as Diane re-emerged from the back room, he considered Miranda had grabbed his hand to get him to regain focus and to silence their talk so Diane couldn't hear.

Diane reclaimed her post at the front desk.

"He's not back there."

"Maybe he called in sick?" said Miranda.

"I'd know that."

"Can you reach him on his cell phone?"

Diane unwrapped a piece of gum and shoved it into her mouth while fumbling with her cell phone. When she got a handle on her multitasking, she hit a speed-dial number on the phone.

The three of them waited for someone to answer, but the effort was futile.

"Is it normal for him not to answer?" Miranda asked.

"He usually answers on the first ring."

Miranda placed her business card on the counter.

"It's important we get this sorted out so we can bring closure to the victim's family," she said. "And the people of Clearwater also deserve to know if they can trust their news source."

Then she sidestepped Jack, who hadn't expected the discussion to end so abruptly, and moved toward the door.

"Jack, do you know where Jeff lives?" Miranda asked.

"He has a place on the lake."

"Let's see if their stories align," said Miranda.

"I'm sure he'll tell you the same thing, that the print is exactly as Jack told him," said Diane.

Miranda stopped mid-stride. She turned from Jack to gaze at Diane.

"You just accused Detective Calaway of lying," said Miranda.

"No I didn't. I didn't say he lied."

"Doubting his word while we're standing here is a direct challenge to his authority and integrity as an officer. That's calling him a liar."

She moved away from the door and gently nudged Jack aside as she approached the counter.

Diane stepped back.

"Normally, I wouldn't care what you said about him or me, but we've been gaslighted and kept silent about it for so long that trust in law enforcement is becoming eroded. So I can't stay silent anymore," Miranda stated.

"What are you talking about?" Diane asked.

"We don't need to escalate this," said Jack. "Let's talk to Jeff."

"She's exactly the type of person we need to start confronting," said Miranda. "People like her challenge our authority, and when we walk away, they misinterpret our tolerance for weakness, reinforcing their crazy logic that we're weak. It endangers us."

Miranda stayed where she was and stared directly at Diane.

"You put on a good front acting as though you respect Detective Calaway," said Miranda. "And it seems like you and your paper trusted him and his press releases for years, and Jack had no complaints until today. So what's different about today and this press release? Why are you turning against him now? Did you talk to someone who changed your opinion of him? Did you hear Jack and Jeff's conversation about a body being found?"

"I wasn't here when Jack stopped by, but we printed the truth. Everyone is saying environmentalists killed this guy," said Diane.

"But you're a paper people trust to inform them that's now making accusations without proof that it was an environmentalist. You're not a stylist at the salon gossiping while cutting someone's hair," said Miranda. "Global Econ Mining has a lot to gain here. And it looks like *The Chronicle* could stand to use some money for a remodel, so maybe you or Jeff did the killing to help the mining company's cause. You could just as easily be the murderer as an environmentalist."

Miranda paused to let Diane process all she'd said.

But Diane kept chewing and popping her gum. Her blank expression implied they move on from considering her or Jeff as killers or that they'd done anything wrong by accepting money from the mining company to cover for them.

"Assuming Jack isn't lying to me because he took an oath to uphold the law, who else had privileged information that a person may or may not have been murdered by an environmentalist?" said Miranda. "And I don't think that's you or Jeff; otherwise, I'd arrest you right now. So where'd you hear it from first?"

"From the public. Everyone's been saying it's most likely an environmentalist."

Diane's blank expression caused Miranda to close her eyes momentarily and think again about how Aruba's warm blue waters made her feel when she'd gone there on a brief vacation. She also always remembered the feeling of surfing when she was younger. She tried to hold onto those feelings of normalcy.

Jack felt himself sweat from the intensity heating up between the two women. Seeing two women arguing captured his attention, regardless of what they were discussing.

"Newspapers and their staff are supposed to base information on credible sources," said Miranda, snapping from her trance. "Did Jack tell you the condition of the body?"

"He didn't have to. We knew the body was mutilated," said Diane. "We heard he had something cut onto his head."

"Who told you that?"

"Everyone."

"Those are details that only people at the murder scene would know, so you're accusing everyone of murder, yet your paper is only singling out environmentalists? I want to know who told you the victim had cuts on his forehead."

"I heard it from multiple people, not from any single person."

"Give us a name."

"I don't have one. It's a rumor that's circulating."

Diane's complete ignorance shocked Miranda, and she continued her scolding. "Newspapers that publicly accuse a person of a crime because everyone says it's true without providing facts can be sued for libel and defamation, as they should be. Do you even think of the people you could be hurting by printing lies? Or the time and resources it takes to disprove them?"

"That's Jeff's call," said Diane. "He's the one with the journalism degree."

"But he isn't here, and you're reinforcing the lies about Jack and environmentalists, which can damage their reputations and endanger them. Do you not see any problem with the way in which you received the information about an environmentalist being involved or the condition of the body?"

The intensity was building in Miranda's eyes, and it appeared to cause Diane to finally slow down and give the question some thought.

"There's a large mining company looking at the area," said Miranda. "Have you in any way been asked to cover up this murder for them?"

Diane pushed a lump down in her throat.

"No one told us to name anyone. It's common knowledge environmentalists are violent people and that they're responsible. They ram ships, destroy property."

"Some of them do. It's usually a last resort when they can't get their point across to the unreachable who don't care about the lasting damage they do to the planet. Do you expect people to sit by quietly if they discover someone is helping sneak through an open-pit mine into a pristine area that belongs to the people? Jack, do you know any violent environmentalists around here?"

"There's Trenton Fuller, but he's not violent."

"Does he have a record?"

"No."

"Are there any others you can think of who we should bring in and question for having a history of violence that we can link to this death?"

"No."

"Is there any reason we should investigate Trenton Fuller?"

"He's never done anything."

"Have you seen any evidence of violence from environmentalists around here?"

"If you're referring to protesters, they've all been peaceful so far," said Jack.

"But they won't be when they bring the violent ones in to halt the progress of this mining company," Diane interrupted.

Miranda's face erupted into shades of red like an instant sunburn. The idea that saving the environment was halting progress was a talking point that never made sense to her. But even worse was helping and defending a company with a destructive international history like Global Econ. She didn't know how to explain to Diane that she was most likely a front helping them cover up the murder of David Willis, or maybe it wouldn't even matter to her. She decided this time she'd let Diane have the final say. Within a few seconds, the color in Miranda's cheeks dissipated from bright red to pink, and her face turned to a look of pity and even of admiration, the way a teacher would look at a student who, no matter what, couldn't see the lesson or beyond the lies or anger they were caught in.

"Have Jeff call Jack when he comes in," said Miranda. Then she turned and disappeared out the door.

Miranda was getting into the car when Jack came outside. She reached for the button on the radio to turn on public talk radio. When she heard the day's topic about possibly impeaching politicians for soliciting help from foreign enemies to get elected, she turned it off again. She was trying to ignore the things that were out of her control. She sometimes wondered if anything she had done in her life had made a difference. Therapists had told her that avoiding thinking about the world's problems would help decrease her anxiety and anger. But pretending problems in the world didn't exist, or that they weren't hers to fix, never did help relax her and made her even more angry and frustrated. She believed such advice to ignore reality was childish and dangerously naive.

Jack took his spot in the passenger seat.

"That could have gone better," he said. "I probably should have been taking notes."

"The truth about what happened to David Willis is being buried, and Diane is perfectly happy to go along with it, even though she doesn't know why they killed him," said Miranda. "And that's dangerous because how do you know the lies can't come back to bite you in the butt if you refuse to see why they're hiding the killing? Either they're completely ignorant about what Global Econ is doing, or they're sensible and too afraid to say anything because if they do, they could also end up with something inscribed on their foreheads. Do you have this Jeff person in your phone contacts?"

"I don't have his personal number, but I know where he lives on the lake."

"I'd like to live on a lake too. Maybe we should bury our heads in the sand and get rich by joining in on the corruption."

Jack grinned at what he thought was an attempt at humor, but Miranda did not smile.

Miranda pushed the button to start the car. Her breathing had gradually de-escalated to the point where she could feel the soothing Northwoods air fill her lungs. She was familiar with the Midwest and the purity of the land, but she preferred being near the ocean in California, where she saw more progressive attitudes. But because of her roots, part of her was upset about the increased anger and confusion she'd witnessed recently in the Midwest.

"Jeff could also be printing their sensationalized version of the killing to sell newspapers because it's what the public wants to hear, which keeps them selling subscriptions," Miranda added. "It's a popular change in journalism from the intended meaning behind freedom of the press and freedom of speech. But I'm betting someone is paying them to feed the public a favorable viewpoint of this mining company and a negative one toward environmentalists while covering up the murder. It's a perfect smokescreen for whatever this company is after. How else did she know David Willis's forehead had been cut? They've obviously been talking to someone."

Jack was hoping it was all coincidental. But Miranda's argument made too much sense to ignore, and his defense of Diane and Jeff no longer had merit the moment Diane mentioned the cutting of David Willis's forehead. He was impressed by how Miranda's mind worked and was ashamed that he had criticized her earlier about wanting to leave before the case had even begun. It did appear that the paper was being used to lead people away from those responsible for murdering David Willis.

"As a precaution, someone should contact this Trenton Fuller, who's now being dragged into this. I could see some radical who believes the lies they're printing about environmentalists and seeking revenge by carving him up too," said Miranda.

"How much do you know about Trenton?" she asked.

"He's sometimes a target of hate crimes—damaged mailboxes, a smashed windshield, things like that."

Jack's phone vibrated before he could respond to Miranda's silence over the news about the vandalism committed against Trenton. Jack took a moment to read the text.

"It's a link from Bill to another newspaper saying the same things as *The Chronicle*," said Jack.

Miranda could already guess what the paper said, as word of another story about the murder confirmed someone was intentionally leaking information. It proved in her mind again that the murder was a cover-up job. And there was no question it was a concerted effort to spread propaganda to conceal the murderer and make the mining company look favorable. It was just like she'd thought. She questioned if Jack was making any sense of it, but she didn't want to have to explain it to him if he wasn't.

She wanted to press the accelerator, keep driving to the warm gulf waters two thousand miles to the south and avoid any confrontation with criminals altogether. The destination didn't seem quite as impossible to reach when she thought of Aruba in terms of miles instead of the cost of an airplane ticket. But then she always remembered how she'd wished adults had stuck around to stop a drunk teenager from getting into a car and killing her parents. There had to be others like her trapped in a situation where they wished someone would have stayed to help them. It was a memory she could never erase.

She pulled over on the side of the highway, tugged cheaters out of her purse, and put them on.

"I thought FBI agents had to have eyesight like fighter pilots," said Jack. "How can you possibly have cheaters already?"

"After what we just learned, you're going to focus on my eyesight?"

"It seems unusual to me, considering all the rigorous physical requirements you must pass before becoming an FBI agent."

"I'm farsighted, so cheaters help with the small print, and if there's ever something that I physically can't do, I'll let you know."

"I'm sorry," said Jack. "I'm just realizing there's a lot I don't know about the FBI. I didn't mean anything by it."

Miranda checked his eyes for sarcasm as she took Jack's phone from his hand. She interpreted the comment as him being defensive for having been wrong about the paper. But it could also be a good sign if he was genuinely concerned about her eyesight. If he was worried she wasn't physically capable of pulling her weight, maybe he'd be willing to do whatever it took to compensate for her deficiencies. It was an awkward moment that felt like something that happens on a first date when someone blurts something out before boundaries are established and secrets are revealed.

After her silence made its impact, Miranda let the argument go and took a moment to read the small print. When she was finished, she handed Jack's phone back to him.

"Law enforcement officials suspect environmental groups are behind the killing" were the words in the article that stood out to her. The extent of the mining company's cover-up was already as bad as she suspected.

It's too coincidental not to be true, Miranda thought.

"There's no question they own the papers in the area. They're funding and slanting the news to control the narrative about how the public views the killing."

She tucked her cheaters into her hair and turned to confront him.

Jack lost concentration momentarily, distracted by how focused and pretty Miranda looked. And he was glad they were able to move on from accidental insults. He'd never been able to move on so quickly from arguments with his ex-wife. He admired Miranda for not allowing a disagreement to affect how she talked to him moving forward with the case.

"If they can control the disinformation, they also control how the public will view us and an investigation into them, so we have to watch our backs. We need to put the focus on them, so it'd be nice to put a face to whoever's involved in starting the lies because they'll be directly connected to the killer. Besides law enforcement, who'd you say has seen the body?"

"His parents and his fiancé."

"And no one asked you if it was okay to release information?" said Miranda.

"No."

"Do you know where the parents and fiancé are now?"

"They're staying at a hotel on the edge of town."

"We'd better get out there and talk to them and see if anyone has confronted them about getting permission to release names.

Jeff can wait."

"If you were able to see this spreading of misinformation so clearly before you even got here, someone else must be seeing the connection to the mining company other than you and me," said Jack. "We can't be the only ones suspecting them."

"Of course other people see it, but how do they stop it without becoming victims? And you and I have the law on our side, but the law doesn't always work when government officials cash in and defend murderers. That's why I think catching a plane and leaving would be easier."

Miranda tilted her arm to glance at her watch. She remembered seeing a flight on her computer that was leaving at twelve thirty. There was no way she'd make it to the airport now, even if she wanted to.

The frequency with which she checked her watch played into Jack's anxiety. But all he could think of were anxious moments with his ex-wife and how sometimes it was better not to say anything. It was better to pretend that he didn't want to know why Miranda kept wishing she were elsewhere, especially when the truth probably meant she was worried about government officials being involved. It was something she'd been implying all along.

He was happy when his phone vibrated again.

Miranda readjusted her sports bra strap that was cutting into her shoulder.

"Will we ever have a moment to catch our breath?" she said.

"They analyzed the bullet," said Jack. "Hollow core, expandable. The lab says it's from a 270 rifle."

Miranda ran her hands through her brown hair and took a deep breath as she sank back into her leather seat.

"It's going too fast, just like I knew it would, and there's too much information to handle on our own. Cuts have been made to the department, and these big corporations know it. It's deliberate. They have people inside relaxing the laws to pave the way for them while burying us with the burden of proof. Your forensics guy, what was his name?"

"Bill."

"Tell Bill to have someone come up with a list of residents in the area with that caliber of rifle. I wouldn't put it past these people to pin this mess on some unsuspecting, innocent resident and try to get others to believe it. We should be looking for someone with no family or connections who would be an easy target."

"A 270 is a common hunting caliber," said Jack. "It could be anybody around here."

"Then narrow the focus. Tell Bill to contact Trenton Fuller to see if he has a 270 registered to him. And if he does, someone needs to talk to him and bring him in to protect him."

CHAPTER
Five

THE MIND BEHIND IT

"Bill is on board," said Jack. "That's all I heard before I lost him."

Jack was often puzzled by why cell reception wasn't more reliable in Clearwater than it was. He had read that a certain block of politicians who held power in the state hadn't designated any money to improve the situation even though most of the population had asked for it. He wondered if Miranda would agree with him or think he was crazy in thinking there seemed to be a political conspiracy to keep the area of Clearwater off the grid. He questioned if they should be driving his truck instead of her car because at least it contained a police radio so they would have more reliable communication.

"We're being cautious about Trenton, but if setting him up is their plan, confronting him also lets them know we're on to it," said Miranda. "I'm glad Bill understood. Without him, it feels like you and I are stranded on an island. And it's a long swim to the mainland without any assistance."

She remembered the first time she'd made the comment about people not living on islands when she'd discovered the body on the beach when she was thirteen. She thought about that day from time to time and the rift it had caused between her and her aunt. Aunt Rita didn't like seeing her dragged into a dangerous world. But the way Miranda saw it, she was already surrounded by it.

"I stressed to him that Trenton isn't a suspect," said Jack. "But maybe I should text him so he knows what I meant by bringing him in."

"Why would you need to text him? They don't have anything to arrest him on. And you said Bill is trustworthy."

"He is, but it's the others in the department who sometimes have minds of their own that I worry about. We're not always on the same page. But I'm sure Bill will get it done."

"There shouldn't be an issue if your department follows the law."

"I know how some of the guys talk about educated people like Trenton, but Bill isn't one of them, so I shouldn't have said anything. He'll pull through."

But Miranda wondered now if the bias that Diane at the newspaper exhibited against environmentalists and Trenton had also infected Jack's department. But even if the message had gotten jumbled, or if Trenton had a history of being treated unfairly, it'd be ridiculous to think the department would accuse him of the murder. It was too foolish to even consider, and she and Jack had to keep moving forward.

Jack's stomach began to growl, so to silence it so Miranda wouldn't hear it, he tightened the muscles in his abdomen and pressed his elbow into his side. As he tried convincing himself Bill would have no trouble telling the others that Trenton wasn't a suspect and that he was to be protected, he wondered how quickly an ulcer could form.

"As we get deeper into this case, people you once were able to trust will start making choices that probably won't coincide with the law. So we have to be ready for it. And it's important we don't forget to take care of ourselves," said Miranda. "Because we're making waves, we'll be drawing unwanted attention to ourselves. One of the reasons I wanted you along with me goes back to what Diane alluded to. If people like her are willing to sacrifice an environmentalist and the truth behind the brutal killing of a biologist to get what suits them, then they'll likely be willing to attack us for trying to expose the truth. I'm not just talking about verbal attacks, either. We need to be mindful of locals who don't want us going after this company, no matter their title."

Her concern redirected Jack's attention away from his growling belly and to the task before them.

"Bill stands with us. Although Diane obviously sides with the mine, I think she's harmless," said Jack. "And we don't even know for sure yet if the mining company is behind it."

"We'll know for sure soon enough."

Miranda checked her cell phone, but she only had one bar.

Jack silently agreed that if it turned out the mining company was responsible, other supporters in the community could pose a bigger, more realistic threat to them than Diane. Even though he'd been suspicious of the mining company's involvement the moment he'd turned over David Willis's body, he still didn't want to accept the possibility that Miranda could be right about any of it.

"Because the state land use office isn't contacting you," said Miranda, "when we get reception, one of us should contact the EPA and The Nature Conservancy, although their impact is becoming less relevant as mining lobbyists keep up their attacks. We need answers about what David Willis might have been looking for within the state park's boundaries."

"How about we call in more agents to help with more of the legwork," said Jack.

"That's a great idea, but I don't know if we'll get more help."

Jack plucked a mint from its plastic container and closed the lid. He didn't think to offer one to Miranda because his mind was still focused on her comment.

"I like *James Bond* and *Mission Impossible* spy thrillers as much as anyone when one or two people solve everything and save the world on their own," said Jack. "But we're talking about you and me now. If no one from your department will help us while we're in the field, there are serious holes in our justice system."

He'd said it half-heartedly. But as he waited for a response, Miranda didn't interrupt the quiet. The silence suggested maybe he'd touched upon one of the secrets she was guarding.

"If no one is helping, you're implying there's a breakdown of the justice system at the federal level," said Jack.

"I've been trying to tell you that all federal oversight departments have taken a hit. Haven't you been paying attention to how the laws and oversight agencies under this particular administration are being eroded?"

"Like others, I don't notice things until they impact me. And you can't be the only one out of thousands of agents who feels you still have an obligation to serve the law. When will we know if we're going to be ignored?"

"When I call and ask for help, but it's too early for that. We have to hold off making calls until we really need them. That's why I'm hoping your department will step up and help."

Jack thought of possible complications within his department ensuring Trenton's safety.

Miranda kept staring ahead at the road and the scenery.

"Forget law enforcement for a moment. Suppose something like a corporate takeover of this state park is what we're witnessing," Jack added. "How are these people at the mining company going to deal with the destruction of the area's tourism industry? The community would never allow it to happen, so maybe we are overthinking this entire case."

They were approaching the hotel on the east end of town near Highway 43, which curved around to the north.

"Clearwater residents are already being trained to believe that the mining operation will bring in a lot more revenue than tourism," said Miranda. "There's a reason why the papers are ignoring your facts and attacking an environmentalist who supports nature and recreational state parks. You thought I was apprehensive about this case because of my inexperience. It turns out maybe I'm not the inexperienced one."

Jack rubbed at the whiskers on his cheek and chin. He opened his mouth in preparation for a good comeback, but he couldn't think of any way to refute or disprove anything she'd said.

When they entered the hotel lobby where David Willis's parents and fiancé were staying, it looked like a vast and elegant banquet hall or dance hall, and the floor was virtually vacant. Groups of three and five plants were strategically placed in the lobby's corners. Black imitation leather couches lined the perimeter among the plants. Jack stopped at the edge of the diamond-patterned black and gold floor. In the background was a fake, rushing waterfall. The woman at the front desk rushed off to unlock the door to the pool for another guest.

"Do you know what room they're in?"

"Three-seventeen."

"Get some coffee so you can stay awake," said Miranda. "And grab a donut and some fruit. And I hope I'm wrong about how I think my boss will react if we need help."

Jack stopped abruptly before continuing to the breakfast area. He had already been alarmed by how Diane back at *The Chronicle* had covered for Jeff. He'd also had reason to be concerned for Trenton's safety and his and Miranda's. And now Miranda brought up again the uncertainty of gaining support.

She was waiting with her hands folded in front of her near the elevator for him to return.

The way she looked at him from across the room while patiently waiting calmed him.

"If you're concerned already that this is as bad as it seems, then we'd better call your people to confirm if we're going to get backup," said Jack.

He blew on his coffee, then took a cautious sip.

"I know you're concerned it's only the two of us, Jack. Right now, key people at the bureau are being re-appointed, so I'm hoping they'll get things sorted out and be there for us when we need them," said Miranda. "I wish I could tell you more, but I don't have anything else."

She placed her finger on the button that kept the elevator door open.

"Are you ready for this?" she said.

"No. Nothing ever makes you ready to meet mourning family members," said Jack. "I've been on scene of enough accidents to know that."

He was still hoping Miranda would clarify why she thought more of her FBI people weren't coming.

He was startled when Miranda grabbed his hand, squeezed it, then let go of it. Jack noted that it was the second time she'd done it.

"What was that for?" he asked.

"For support."

"I'm glad you're worried about me, but I'm fine," said Jack.

"It wasn't for you. You're still confident that someone is going to step in and relieve you of your responsibility. But I'm counting on you to pull through because there may not be anyone else."

When he felt the delicate touch of her hand, Jack wondered how she'd ever passed the brutal fitness portion of the FBI training program, but she had somehow done it, even with her failing eyesight. If she had physical strength, it certainly wasn't bulging from her arms or wrists, although he could see she was in great shape. But after her comment about there being no one else and talking about the shakeup at the FBI, he decided now that her touching his hand at *The Chronicle* was probably done out of fear that he wouldn't step up when she needed him to. He could sense the color drain from his face.

They stood in the elevator and watched the white numbers above the closed doors light up.

When the elevator slowed to a stop, and the door opened, Jack let Miranda out of the elevator first and followed closely behind her to the end of the hallway. He tried not to stare at her attractive shape, but his eyes were drawn to her.

Miranda whispered, "We get in, and we get out. I can handle

mutilated bodies, and I can even handle being lied to, but I'm not good at meeting with families after something like this happens."

"I don't like it either, but I've already met with the family, so do you want me to do it?"

"I want to be there with you. I lost my parents when I was six, so I've seen the other side of this. I want to be there for them."

"You really lost your family?"

"It happened when I was young. A teenager, with no license, drunk, swerved into our lane and hit us head-on. He survived. They're always the ones who survive. He never apologized, never showed a hint of remorse. I ended up living with my aunt in California."

"If this makes you relive it, it's no bother for me to go in alone."

"I'm telling you about it because I thought it might offer some insight into my crazy behavior aside from the anxiety of this case. There's a little more to the story in terms of finding a body when I was young, but it's what made me want to set the world straight, and when I was younger, I used to think I'd be able to. Now, I think the world is too broken to fix, and that's why I talk about running away."

Jack wasn't sure why she opened up to him, but he felt warm inside when she had.

"I'm hoping they'll be able to give us a name," said Miranda.

The door to the suite was propped open by a clump of damp hotel towels, and a breeze was blowing in from the balcony. White curtains were swaying in the wind.

Miranda knocked and called out for Mr. and Mrs. Willis.

Mrs. Willis came out of the bathroom. Her eyes and cheeks were red, and she had a Kleenex in one hand and reading glasses folded in the other. She wasn't wearing any makeup and was dressed in a white blouse and black pants. She was barefoot.

Miranda tried not to stare as she introduced herself. Knowing Mrs. Willis and Jack had met once before, she made a quick reintroduction.

Mrs. Willis's eyes sparkled, and the pitch of her voice lifted momentarily when she asked if they'd found something or made any arrests.

"Not yet. We need to run some evidence by you," said Miranda. "Is your husband here? Would he like to sit in on the conversation?"

"He and Amanda, David's fiancé, went for a walk," said Mrs. Willis. The optimism had vanished from her face. "Should we wait for them?"

"There's no need. I only have a few quick questions so I know if we're on the right track."

Miranda sat in a chair and placed a digital voice recorder on a nearby desk. Jack stood behind her. They were careful to give Mrs. Willis her space.

"First of all. I'm terribly sorry for your loss," said Miranda. "But I'll get to the point as to why we're here. Two newspapers have released articles about your son's death ahead of the investigation. One of the articles named your son, who he was working for, and possible people or groups that might be responsible. It seems to me they tried to make it sound like an official police report when it wasn't. We're trying to figure out who the newspapers interviewed or where they got permission to release the information."

"They probably got it from this mining company, Global Econ. They contacted me after I left the morgue," said Mrs. Willis. "They told me what happened and asked if it was okay if they released information to the newspapers."

"The company told you your son had been killed and asked you if they could release information?" said Miranda.

"Was that wrong?" said Mrs. Willis with a hint of defensive indignation. "They seemed concerned."

"So they already knew yesterday before anyone else that something had happened to your son?" Miranda clarified.

"Apparently. They thought getting the information out would help with an investigation."

"But those people aren't your son's employer," said Jack. "So why would they have contacted you, and how would they know what happened to David?"

Mrs. Willis tilted her head in confusion.

"I guess they wanted to help because I'm his mother. They told me they already had a suspect. Someone named Trent or Trenton. So maybe you should be looking for him."

Miranda gauged Jack's reaction to see whether they'd heard Mrs. Willis correctly. Then she redirected her attention to Mrs. Willis.

"Did you have a connection with this mining company before yesterday?" she asked.

"No."

Miranda took out her phone, opened the note-taking app, and began punching in her thoughts. She typed the words *New-berry Press and who owns it?* And then she typed, *Global Econ—They had him killed. Why????* She bolded the last part she typed—**Purposely taunting the family!**

"Do you remember who you spoke with at Global Econ Mining?" she continued.

"A man named Ethan Richards. He seemed concerned."

Even though she was sure Mrs. Willis had spoken loudly enough for the voice recorder to pick it up, Miranda also recorded the name.

"David works for the state, yet the mining company called you. Why would a company your son doesn't work at be calling you?" Miranda asked again. She thought if she and Jack kept asking, the realization that the mining company was involved in her son's death would sink in.

"I suppose David must have listed us as emergency contacts."

When Mrs. Willis didn't catch on, Jack folded his arms in frustration and disbelief. He circled the room for a moment.

"Did your son ever work with anyone regularly in the field?" Miranda asked.

"He never mentioned anyone."

"Would this Ethan Richards' number be on your list of recent calls?"

"I don't know," Mrs. Willis said.

"Do you mind if I look?"

Mrs. Willis's hands shook as she unlocked her iPhone, looked through the messages, and passed it to Miranda.

"It must be this one," she said. "The others are family."

Miranda selected the one Mrs. Willis pointed out to her. She sent it to her phone and did a quick Google search to make sure it was the correct number. The image of a tall, angular man in a gray suit and red striped tie with the name of Ethan Richards popped up on the site along with a bio. She briefly looked over his title and information.

His title read Land Acquisitions.

"Did you ever meet Ethan Richards?"

"No," said Mrs. Willis. "But he gave you both a lead, something about someone named Trenton or environmentalists being behind it."

"It wasn't an environmentalist or a man named Trenton who killed your son, but the people who did it want you to believe it was so you help spread the lie about who really did it. Don't talk to Ethan Richards or anyone else from the mining company unless we're with you," said Miranda. "Would you say your son was an ethical person?"

"Of course. And he was always curious. He took a lot of photos and was always doing puzzles. He loved science and nature. And he liked working for the state even though he wasn't always happy with the pay, but when student loans come due, you take what you can find. And I told him to tough it out until something better came along. That may have been a mistake."

"Do you know what type of accounts he had or if he stored photos in an online account?" Miranda asked.

"That's something you'd have to ask Amanda."

"What about passwords?"

"She'd have to help you with that."

"Have her contact Jack or me," said Miranda as she handed Mrs. Willis back her phone along with her business card. "And please have her send us any passwords for anywhere he might have uploaded photos."

Miranda grabbed the video voice recorder and got up.

Before Jack realized what she was doing, she walked from the room.

"We'll get back to you again when we have more information," said Jack. "Once again, please accept my condolences for your loss."

He closed the door behind him on his way out.
Moving down the hallway, he texted something, sent it, then met Miranda in the elevator. But neither of them felt like speaking, so they stood there in silence, watching the numbers count down from three to one.

Miranda finally spoke when they reached the lobby.

"Get a counselor down here for the family," she said.

"I already texted for one to be sent," said Jack.

"I knew this case was gonna be bad, but these people have no soul, attacking the family the way they have. I need to figure out what we should do next, so don't bother me while I think."

They drove with the windows down after leaving the parking lot.

Jack leaned to his right side with his butt raised off the seat, sticking his head out the window in the breeze so he could stay awake. He had no idea where they were going next. And for the moment, he didn't care. He filled his lungs with the fresh air, and he appreciated taking a moment from talking about the case. Miranda took a look at his butt before he brought his head inside the car again and sat down. Even though he may not have been the most versed in navigating such a difficult case, he seemed normal to her. He wasn't pretentious, egotistical, mean, or terribly complex to the point where he might be manipulative. Even though he was older, he didn't act like it. Jack was rare.

"They had knowledge of David's death before anyone else, and they set up Trenton Fuller," said Miranda. "Did you hear everything she said?"

"Yes."

"So the killer reported back to this Ethan Richards. I suspect he's the guy who ordered the hit. And on top of all that, why isn't the state returning your phone calls? Unless they knew what David was sent out to do and were involved themselves. Either they're complicit or too terrified to come forward after hearing what was done to a colleague."

"Then this is exactly like you said," said Jack. "So now is when we should bring in the SWAT team and your friends at the bureau and close in on this guy. She gave us enough information to bring him in and question him about how he knew about the death before anyone else. He obviously had something to do with it."

"That's a great idea. But when we bring Ethan Richards in for questioning or arrest him, and his team of lawyers step in and tell him not to incriminate himself because we have nothing solid to entrap him with or bargain with, then what? You still don't understand the extent of what we're involved in."

Then she looked ahead at the road, and Jack could sense she wasn't finished. She slowed the car and pulled into a gravel driveway that led nowhere.

Jack put his coffee cup in the holder and crossed his arms. He knew from experience that it was serious whenever a woman pulled a car over to talk. He instinctively assumed a defensive position by folding his arms before the car slowed.

Miranda shoved the shifter forward, and the car abruptly stopped.

"Maybe if we're lucky, a judge would grant us the use of wiretaps so we can listen in on Ethan Richards," said Miranda. But this guy knew law enforcement would find his name if anyone talked with the family. Because he was so bold about not trying to hide, it should tell you how comfortable he is in thinking he'll never be questioned or arrested. That means he knows people. We'll be lucky to walk away with our jobs if we start digging into this, not to mention our lives if we decide to push it where we both know it needs to go."

"So we've gone as far as we can," said Jack, daring her to agree with him. "Is that what you're saying?"

"This is where sensible detectives would find the gunman and end the case, but then Ethan Richards goes unpunished because there's no way he tailed David into the woods and pulled the trigger. But even though he might not have killed him, he most likely ordered it. And the people at this mining company know proving his involvement will require us getting help that will be too difficult to get."

Jack ran his fingers through his hair because it was all he knew to do. Along with the heavy burden placed upon them, he sensed that meeting with Mrs. Willis had brought back Miranda's feelings of losing her parents.

"But doing what's smart doesn't undo the pain this guy has caused, so I can't just walk away and leave the country even though I want to. And leaving doesn't help anyone, and I have to believe there are more people here than you and the Willis family who want help. Because of the money that's most likely fueling these people, we'll need a miracle to get these people. We need some leverage. Something they missed."

Miranda closed her eyes. Her breathing slowed, and she could feel the tense lines on her forehead and under her eyelids relax. She remembered stepping on the sun-baked sand at the beach when she was young. She remembered when she stood firmly on the surfboard and rode the wave all the way in for the first time, shortly before she'd stumbled across a dead body that had washed up on shore.

Jack was about to tell Miranda that she was right for wanting to see the case through to the end, even if she was worried about receiving assistance from her department. Jack was sure the FBI would come through when the time came.

As he was about to speak, Miranda's eyes opened suddenly with clarity.

"There's always private land butting up to state parks," she said. "No one saw the killer in the park because he didn't enter there."

Jack unfolded his arms and sighed at how quickly her mind shifted, forcing him to keep up with her.

"I was trying to think of other access points this morning," said Jack. "But I was so busy, and only one comes to mind."

"Where is that?"

"The Lewis family has land that joins up with the park property. The house sits back, probably half a mile away. The family has owned it for over a century."

"How well do you know them?"

"I don't know them at all except by name. I see Mrs. Lewis in town once or twice a year, but I've never talked to her."

"Is there a Mr. Lewis?" Miranda asked.

"I think he passed a few years back. It used to be a big family, but I think Doris is the only one left."

"What do you know about her and the property?"

"I heard the state wanted to buy the property from the family years ago to include it with the park, but at the time, the family refused. Doris lives at the old homestead. She must be in her eighties now."

"What's she like?"

"People say she's mean and guarded. I've heard stages of dementia might be setting in," said Jack. "I've also heard rumors of her painting landscapes of flowers."

"Is she protective of her property?"

"She's never called to complain about trespassers, if that's what you mean. From what I've heard, she doesn't like drawing attention to herself."

"Maybe it's time for us to meet her."

CHAPTER
Six

THE ORCHID PAINTER

"I keep thinking about Ethan Richards," said Jack. "I don't think I've seen anyone ever treat anyone like he did Mrs. Willis and her family."

"People like Ethan Richards have been around forever, so his behavior is nothing new," said Miranda. "But what is new is that people like him are showing up more frequently, and their behavior is tolerated."

"If this guy is for real and he really is well connected, we're in way over our heads. Have you ever thought we might be walking into an ambush? Why don't they simply kill the both of us right now?"

"You just thought of that now?"

They'd traveled toward Doris Lewis's place, mentally preparing themselves for what they might find.

"For all they know, we're two incompetent detectives, and they're going to trust we won't make any connection to them," said Miranda.

"I've also thought about what you said about losing your parents at a young age. It makes perfect sense why you would want to work in law enforcement."

"I didn't tell you because I wanted your pity. I told you so you'd understand why I punish myself by going after these people, even if I have to do it alone."

"Maybe you want to do this alone to prove a point about being good enough and not needing help."

Miranda recalled therapists from her past raising that very question about self-acceptance in the absence of her parents. She thought the comment was bold but insightful coming from Jack.

"You make observations not many people even think of, Jack. But I'm right on this one. Unless crime directly impacts them, no one is going to help us pursue a case of probable cause against someone like Ethan Richards or a company as large as Global Econ when they'll most likely be sued for attempting something so foolish. Do you want to drop out of this case and take a vacation?" Miranda asked, half joking.

"This area is my home; it's my job to defend it," said Jack.

"Then, since we're still committed, venturing off on our own in search of physical evidence is the only real chance we have. Is your gun loaded?" Miranda asked.

"The clip is always full, but I never put one in the chamber," said Jack. "I never wanted to shoot someone accidentally."

"Normally, I'd say that's a great idea. But as long as I'm with you, and since there's a new world order beating on Clearwater's door that's now impacting both of us, start putting a damn shell in the chamber," said Miranda.

The urgency in her voice was enough to convince Jack he needed to stop doubting her. He was beginning to feel like he was at the back of a train rounding a corner headed toward an ominous destination, and there was no way off. Once the Camry stopped, he would slide the smooth action of his pistol back and put a bullet in the chamber.

The gravel driveway seemed to go on forever. Long grass grew between the paths left by tires. A "Hollywood driveway," some people called it. But there was no glitter or glamour to it.

No stone or concrete or pavement. Only gravel and grass accented by trees and sky—indicators of a simple life.

Jack felt his gun under his jacket as they bumped along, the wispy grass dragging along the Camry's undercarriage. The banter between the two was losing its innocent charm—he had never pulled his gun on anyone before. And then he remembered how much his ex-wife hated that he was a detective, and not because she was afraid of losing him. She often empathized and sided with people he had arrested and helped prosecute, people who needed to be held accountable for their stupid behavior. As the likelihood of a face-off with armed criminals seemed to increase with each passing hour he spent with Miranda, Jack thought back to this morning when she had brought up looking after his son. He started thinking about a confrontation with a gunman and what it would mean for Aiden's future if his father were lost or injured. Thinking about it made him anxious.

He texted Aiden at school. *How is your day going? Text me when you get this.*

Jack gripped his phone, waiting for it to vibrate. He hoped for an immediate response, but it was like waiting to be told he was good at detective work. "Teenagers," he said. Mine is supposed to be different from the rest, he thought.

"You're holding that phone tight like it's a lifeline," said Miranda.

"It's my son."

"Is he alright?"

"The more time I spend with you, the more real this thing gets. I was thinking about what you said about his safety, so I texted him. It could be a while before I hear back. Sometimes it feels like I've never had anyone who would listen to my concerns. And after everything I've seen these last couple of days and talking with you about my son, I'm rethinking my relationship with him."

Miranda felt a breakthrough moment had just occurred with Jack. She could feel the lines on her forehead that had taken hold again begin to lift momentarily.

The old farmhouse appeared when the two detectives rounded a corner in the driveway. It looked like it hadn't had a coat of paint since the forties or fifties, but somehow the structure looked solid. The grass was mowed, and the shrubs were well groomed. The Woodland home was probably a Sears, Roebuck house purchased from the catalog over a century ago. And at this point in her life, what did a coat of paint matter? At some point, Doris Lewis realized the house was sure to outlast her, so what else was there to do except make raspberry and blackberry jam, paint landscapes on canvas from time to time, and sit outside and watch storms roll in from the west?

"I would have gotten around to coming out here, but I focused on questioning people in the park. It's been a busy morning," said Jack.

"You don't have to explain," said Miranda. "And if I've been rude or condescending, I didn't mean it. It's my way of handling stress because I know this is where things can get serious. If Mrs. Lewis is as old as you say, it might not matter if we're here or not. Her mind might be too far gone to help, so this is a long shot."

Doris knew something important was stirring when she saw the black Toyota Camry meandering up the drive. She already suspected something was up, having seen an occasional helicopter circling overhead yesterday afternoon. Usually, it meant that a hiker or climber had fallen in the park close to the lake and needed to be life-flighted to a trauma or emergency center. But the air traffic yesterday seemed much closer to her home than normal.

She thought of not answering the knock at the door, but even at seventy-nine, she was still part of this world, though few people in the area acknowledged it. Owning land and her health were the only factors that kept her in the game.

Mrs. Lewis swung open her front door.

"You're wasting your time. I'm not interested in selling," said Doris without waiting for the intruders to speak.

"We're not interested in your land, Mrs. Lewis," said Miranda.

"There are only two reasons why people ever drive out here. One is to see if I'm dead so someone can have the land, and two is to see if I'll sell before I'm dead. I like seeing the disappointed look on their faces when they realize I can still form coherent sentences."

"A man was killed late yesterday afternoon in the state park that borders your land," said Miranda. "We're wondering if you saw or heard anything suspicious."

Doris, a woman once tall and straight but now of medium height due to her slumped shoulders, stepped in front of the screen door. The force of the steel spring sucked the screen door back against its frame.

"You think someone accessed the park from my property?"

"It's possible."

"Hikers sometimes come across the property, but not very often. Why do you think the man was killed and that it wasn't an accident or a suicide?"

"The evidence points in another direction," said Miranda.

"Evidence you can't talk about?"

"We're unable to discuss that with you at this time. But can you verify where you were yesterday?"

"I was inside painting, trying to recreate a landscape," said Doris. "But I'm flattered you think I'm still able enough to be considered a suspect in a killing."

"The people I interviewed at the park yesterday afternoon said they didn't hear or see anything suspicious," said Jack. "So we're wondering if someone may have walked across your property to target the victim."

Miranda said, "We hate bothering you. I'm Detective Fetting with the FBI, and you probably know Detective Calaway from town."

Doris immediately directed her gaze toward Jack.

"Raymond Calaway was your grandfather?" she asked.

"Yes," said Jack.

Miranda was surprised by the enthusiastic and even respectful tone of Doris's question. "I have a UTV out in the barn," said Doris. "Let me switch out my clothes and put jeans on, and we'll ride to where the land borders the park."

Before she went inside, she threw Jack a set of keys.

"And when I come out, I'm bringing a gun with me. Who's to

say a killer isn't still in the area?"

"What caliber do you have, Doris?" asked Miranda.

"A six millimeter. And no, I didn't kill anyone with it. It was a gift from my late husband."

"We're already armed."

"You'll need a rifle if someone is shooting at you from a distance," suggested Doris.

Miranda nodded. "Good point. Then either Jack or I will hold on to it. Do you mind if we check out the barn while we wait?"

"You probably should. It'd be a great place for someone to hide, especially after the rain last night."

After Doris disappeared inside, Jack said, "Let me first text Bill and the others to let them know where we're at in case we go missing."

"Do you have a bulletproof vest?"

"Yes. But I left it in my truck."

"We should both start wearing them. If I had to start this case over with someone else, I really would leave for Aruba. And even as naive as you are, part of me might miss you, Jack."

When they approached the barn, Miranda insisted on going inside first. She slid the heavy wooden door open, and with her gun drawn, she slipped through the narrow opening. Jack followed directly behind her. There was no hayloft where anyone could hide, and the stanchions where the cows were milked years ago had been removed. The barn was empty except for some pigeons, a late sixties light blue Ford Thunderbird convertible in mint condition, and a new red and black UTV with a roll bar, cab, and knobby tires that could tackle the roughest terrain.

Miranda exhaled a sigh of relief and patted Jack on the shoulder with one hand as she holstered her pistol with the other. Then she put her hand on Jack's arm. She second-guessed herself and immediately removed it. Then she lurched forward and hugged him. Jack wasn't expecting it and didn't know how to take it, so he kept his arms at his side and didn't hug her back.

"I should be getting used to it by now, but why the affection?" he asked as Miranda let go.

"Because the barn's clear, and you tolerate all my crazy advice. I know this has been a difficult morning for you, but you're doing well, considering where we started. And you haven't said anything sexually offensive, unlike other guys I've worked with."

Miranda stepped outside.

Jack slid the barn door open the rest of the way so they could bring out the UTV.

When Doris came out of the house and stepped down the front porch steps, she was wearing bluejeans and a flannel shirt. Her six-millimeter rifle was tucked in her arm like she was twenty again, joining Ernest Hemingway on a hunting safari.

Had they been in the suburbs or city, Miranda wouldn't have allowed her to bring the gun along, but she knew life in the country was different. Many newborns had been gifted a gun as the doctor was cutting the umbilical cord, especially from Doris's generation. But the guns were always used for hunting, not for shooting biologists. Still, Miranda and Jack both kept an eye on her.

"Doris," said Miranda, "has there been interest in mining this area in the past?"

"You're asking about that mining company that wants to put an open pit mine twenty miles north of here," said Doris.

"How do you feel about it?"

"Some people say it's probably necessary to help create technology that will reverse climate change if it isn't too late already. But it's going to come at a cost to this area. It'll wreck land values and probably the groundwater, and certainly the landscape. So the people who live here should be the ones who benefit from it and have the most say in how it's done. But that's probably not going to be the case; otherwise, you wouldn't be bothering an old woman for help."

Doris handed Miranda the rifle.

"We should have shown you some identification," said Miranda, displaying her badge.

"Mr. Calaway is in uniform. That's good enough for me."

The UTV had two bucket seats in the front and two in the back. Doris insisted on sitting next to Jack in the front. Miranda sat behind him.

Miranda thought it was sweet how possessive Doris seemed to be of Jack.

For Doris to have a new UTV at her age, she must have some money, Jack thought. He'd never been under the impression that the Lewises had money to spare for luxuries. So it was a bit of a surprise that she had it, but he was grateful she did and that she was allowing them to use it. Jack had always heard there was a bit of mystery surrounding the Lewis family.

Miranda wondered how much she should tell Doris, but names and the fact that David Willis had been killed had already been released in the newspapers anyway. She wasn't going to share anything that people didn't already know.

"David Willis had a biology degree, and he was working in the land use office for the state," Miranda said to Doris, talking loudly over the noise of the engine.

Jack backed his foot off the accelerator so Doris could hear.

"We think David was here scouting out this area, looking for something because he knew the mining company wants to take the state park land. We think the mining company had him killed."

"We don't know anything else because no one is cooperating. At least no one has returned any calls yet," said Jack.

"It doesn't make sense that he'd be doing a casual sweep of the state park if they weren't interested in taking it," said Doris. "The mining company is probably trying to include this entire area with the site to the north, and he knew it, so they probably killed him."

It was obvious to Jack and Miranda that despite her age, Doris was as sharp or sharper than someone sixty years younger. She also seemed more knowledgeable about the mining company's practices than others they'd spoken with.

"What are your thoughts on why a mining company might have had a state employee killed?" said Miranda.

"I'm sure you both already have your suspicions, but I'll play along. First of all, if they really are after this area, it's a state park. And second, even if they could somehow purchase or have the land granted to them, rare plants or animals would endanger a mining operation's ability to get federal permits. They can't get them if an exotic plant or animal is proven to exist in the area, but you both already know this," said Doris.

"Do you know of any such plants or animals on the list?" Miranda asked.

"There used to be calypso orchids here. My generation always knew they were in the valley, but I've read they've become increasingly rare with climate change. I have paintings of them everywhere in my house. But it's been decades since I've gone to the spot where I used to find them."

Miranda's eyes met Jack's in the rearview mirror.

Doris placed her hand on the side of the steering wheel and nudged it to the left when they reached a fork in the path.

"Where are you taking us?" asked Jack.

"We're checking trail cameras. I have them out to watch the wildlife, but every now and then, they capture someone who isn't expecting to have their picture taken."

Jack looked in the rearview mirror again and saw Miranda staring back at him. He now realized what she was after when she'd asked him about Doris's character and personality. "Mean and guarded," which didn't seem like an accurate depiction of Doris at all, suggested Doris was protective of her property and knew about everything happening on it. It was luck that cameras would be placed around the perimeter to photograph wildlife that might also capture trespassers. He was beginning to realize it was how Miranda's mind worked, making her even more attractive.

Under different circumstances, the scenery would have been beautiful—an open grassy prairie on top of a plateau ran to a fence line now buried in wild grape vines that bordered a vast wilderness of tall oaks and towering cedars.

"It's there. Stop," said Doris.

The UTV came to a squeaky halt, and Jack turned off the engine.

Miranda got out first and quickly walked around the front of the vehicle to the deer path in front of them. The path was muddy from the rain, and she walked along it, looking for footprints among the deer tracks. She thought she saw the outline of a boot print. She stooped to touch it, but it was too difficult to tell if it was a human print among the deer hoof imprints that had trampled it. She followed the path in each direction until it turned to prairie grass and cone flowers before giving up on it.

"That must be the valley where David Willis was found?" said Miranda.

She was pointing in the direction where the deer path headed off toward the woods.

"About half a mile away from this point," said Jack.

"There it is," said Doris. But she wasn't looking in the direction Jack and Miranda were.

The two detectives saw Doris pointing at the small rectangular box attached to a cedar tree, concealed behind vines so only the camera's lens was showing.

"How many of these do you have out?" Miranda asked.

"Four. The locals know enough to look out for them, but many of these people coming from the cities aren't aware of them. When my husband was alive, he put them out to watch the deer. Every now and then, I get hikers who wander out of the park. Once, I got pictures of a couple screwing, so that was entertaining. Neither one of them knew what they were doing. We have to pull out the little blue SD card and take it back to the computer."

"A phone will act as the computer, so all we need is a reader, and I always carry one with me. Will the trail cam photos have dates and times on them?" Miranda asked.

"Yes."

"Jack, do you have your phone?"

"Yes, but I don't know why I carry it because I rarely can get ahold of anyone."

She handed him a small black card reader that had a phone cord connected to it.

"Do you know how to download it?" Miranda asked.

"I'm probably better with technology than you are. Go do something productive while I do this," said Jack.

Miranda grinned at how comfortable Jack was becoming at letting her know when he'd had enough of her sometimes overbearing personality.

She noted the proximity of the rustic gravel road they had taken before they got to the driveway leading up to the house. They were far enough away that they couldn't see the barn or the house. And because there was a stand of maple trees between them and the gravel road, Miranda thought it'd be the perfect place for a killer to enter the forest.

"How much traffic do you get on the road, Doris?"

"Except for the mailman, sometimes I don't see a car for several days. Sometimes it seems like a week."

"And Jack, you never sent any detectives or officers to do a sweep of this area from the park side?"

"We searched for evidence within the park in the area where the body was found, and that's it."

Miranda left Doris and Jack to deal with the trail camera as she walked toward the road.

"She seems ambitious," Doris said to Jack.

"She's even smarter than she first seems," said Jack.

"You said your grandfather was Raymond," said Doris.

"Yes. Did you know him?"

"He had a tendency to want to hold back others from doing what he could never do. I'm glad to see you have a mind of your own and broke free from that nonsense. I bet he would have hated to know his grandson went into law enforcement, but that would have been his problem, not yours."

Doris pushed in the side tab and clicked open the front cover on the trail camera. She blew out the ants that had begun building a nest inside. It was a common ritual. How ants found a way inside the sealed camera always puzzled her.

She pushed the blue SD card down and popped it out. Her wrinkled and arthritic hands strained to grasp and pull it from the port. Jack didn't want to insult her by stepping in and speeding up the process by removing the card. Her comment about his grandfather didn't insult him because it confirmed what he'd always heard.

"The EPA has a lot of people in this area angry because of the regulations they put on companies like this mining company," said Doris. "So many of these community members naturally see those government agencies and regulations as job killers. Your grandfather would have been one of them. But if he had thought about others and not only himself, he might have realized that without rules, we'd be a third-world country, drinking polluted groundwater and living with the threat of a company coming in and pushing us out. But that's the problem. So many here only think about themselves, and those are the ones you have to watch out for."

Doris handed him the tiny SD card, and Jack slid it into the reader.

Doris pulled another SD card from her pocket and replaced the one they'd taken.

"I hope I'm wrong, but there are a lot of people here who lack vision who could turn on you if you provide them with the truth about this killing. Watch out for people who've been told this mine is all they have."

When Doris finished speaking, Jack pushed down the lump he felt in his throat.

"We appreciate the help," said Jack.

"You would have appreciated me even more when I was young," said Doris.

When Miranda approached them, she held her phone and was scrolling through images.

"Find anything yet?" Miranda asked.

"Deer pictures, but more images are downloading," said Jack.

"I took some photos of tire tracks that are probably nothing and no one will care about. And Doris," said Miranda, "if anything shows up on the camera, you shouldn't get dragged into this. You're already too involved."

"If anyone is on my camera, then I want to see it," said Doris. "Jack and I were just talking about how it's time some of us started taking a stand against people who wish to drag us into an illegal mining operation with them. And if you two are working alone out here, you're going to need more help."

When image one hundred twenty-seven slid into focus, following deer picture after deer picture, a man appeared on the phone screen. He was walking away from the camera toward the state park. He wore green and brown camouflage and had a gun slung over his shoulder. They couldn't see the man's face.

"It's a hunting rifle," Miranda pointed. "It could be a 270. It looks like a homemade silencer."

"Is he some sort of militia?" said Jack.

"Or a domestic terrorist either hired by the company or inspired by all the hype," said Miranda. "But Ethan Richards knew David Willis had been killed, so we know there's a definite connection between these two. We just have to prove it."

The tip of the rifle was larger in diameter than the rest of the barrel, which indicated a silencer had been screwed onto it. Jack and Miranda knew it was homemade. Despite all the recently relaxed regulations on guns, it was illegal for commercial companies to make silencers for hunting rifles.

"The time on the photo is right, the direction he's walking is correct, and the silencer explains why no one heard it."

"There isn't a jury who wouldn't find him guilty of first degree," said Jack.

"Don't count on it," said Miranda. "If it comes down to him trying to protect whatever secret someone at the mining company doesn't want us to find, he'll have a lot of sympathizers on the side of the mining company." Then she turned to Doris.

"How much of a time delay is there before the camera will take another photo?"

"I think it's set for a minute," Doris responded.

The next photo on the card to download was taken an hour later. It showed the same man walking toward the camera, away from the woods where David Willis was killed. This time he was facing the camera and had the gun slung over his shoulder like he was out for an afternoon stroll. The facial features were easily identifiable.

"Anyone recognize him?" asked Miranda.

"No," said Jack.

"It creeps me out to think he was that close," said Doris.

The man in the photo appeared to be in his forties and slightly overweight. He had short hair and a military-style cut. His face seemed permanently downturned with anger.

"Doris, we'll need the camera for evidence. I'll return it when we're finished," said Miranda.

"I thought maybe we should leave it out here."

"We'll need it for evidence, and I don't anticipate any more traffic coming through this way. I want to do things by the book."

"I understand policy," said Doris.

Miranda snapped photos of the trail camera with her phone.

Holding the phone and card reader, Jack walked to the UTV and sat in the driver's seat. Doris and Miranda climbed into their seats and buckled in.

"We need to get him into the facial recognition database," said Jack.

"We know this isn't a random serial killer, so the public shouldn't be in danger," said Miranda. "So let's make sure we have all the evidence we can find first. Doris, if you're still willing to help, a ride to the other cameras would be appreciated."

They drove off to the south. But the first camera was the only one with anything of use on it. The others contained images of deer and an occasional wandering coyote or wild turkey.

When they arrived back at the house, they left the UTV outside and walked up the steps and into the open dining area at the front of the house.

At the table, Doris poured them ice water and brought out some cake.

"Doris, you don't need to do that. You've done enough," said Miranda.

"I'm at the right place, at the right time to help, and with views toward the FBI and any sort of environmental regulations in this area being shaped the way they are, you're going to need help."

Jack thought it was an interesting comment because it coincided with what Miranda had been telling him about using propaganda to shape people's reality.

"Can we sign into your Wi-Fi to send a message?" he asked.

"It's patchy, but it should work."

"We need to be careful with how we handle this," Miranda cautioned. "If we send this out and someone makes an arrest without first linking this guy to anyone else involved, the chance of him talking and getting everyone who helped design and instigate the murder decreases substantially. And after interviewing Mrs. Willis, we know it doesn't end with this guy."

Doris pulled out a chair at the opposite side of the table and sat.

"Doris, you can't share any of this with anyone," Miranda continued. "We shouldn't even be having this conversation here."

"I have no one to tell. All of my friends are dead. And I'm on your side. My paintings should be enough to convince you of that."

Behind them, they could see another room with pictures of sunsets and flowers on canvas. The colorful lily pad pond patterns looked like attempts to mimic Monet. Pastel colors accenting pink daylilies filled the room. And there were paintings of purple orchids everywhere.

Doris's profile and apparent love for nature didn't match someone who would aid someone in covering up a murder to steal a state park.

"I should make it clear that we're not standing against the idea of mining. It's the practices in this company's recent history that led us to question their involvement in the murder," said Miranda. "Jack, text me the photo so I can send it."

Jack linked the photo to Miranda's phone number.

"Something we haven't thought about is the hole in the theory that David Willis was killed over the discovery of an orchid," said Jack. "The Nature Conservancy would have let the EPA know of any endangered species in the area, and they would have contacted the mining company to say this area is off limits, so why is the mining company still pursuing this area if we're thinking there's a known endangered species here?"

"Bribes," said Miranda.

"Or maybe people think the orchids no longer exist," said Doris. "It's been a while since I've heard of people finding them, but the people who used to pay attention to their numbers were from my generation and are long gone. But I also saw the orchid numbers decline drastically in the seventies, and people stopped looking for them. I haven't been out looking for them in years."

"I hope it's so simplistic that people have lost track of them," Miranda responded. Then Doris got up and left the table.

Having realized Doris had turned out to be a gem of a find, Miranda and Jack both looked satisfied at each other.

"They could have pressured David Willis not to find anything, but they needed him to sign off on it. I'm not judging him anymore about his drinking," said Jack.

Doris returned with an encyclopedia—not an encyclopedia site on the computer, but one of the encyclopedia books from the seventies. Her finger marked a spot near the middle.

"There," she said. "That's how remarkable they are. I have paintings of them throughout the house, but as I said, I haven't been in the woods looking for them in years."

She laid the book on the table and spun it around for them to see. The page displayed a delicate, prehistoric-looking white and purple flower in the shape of an egg.

"The Nature Conservancy must know about them," said Miranda.

"They'd be easy to overlook because in most areas, there never were many to begin with, except this one place," said Doris. "And not everyone is as thorough as the conservancy once was. They could be classified as extinct in this area."

"Then we'll need to look into it for ourselves unless someone shows up and volunteers to do it for us," said Miranda. "I also need to submit an affidavit to see if we can get wiretaps on this Ethan Richards. It'd be easier to get if we can ID this guy in the photo and link him directly to the mining company."

The news of Miranda finally seeking outside help relaxed Jack's stiff posture. It made him wonder if her anxiety and secrecy had been about the bureau's budget being cut or what prevented them from receiving help.

"And it makes sense that David Willis was looking for something, maybe orchids, in the state park because he knew they were looking to mine it," Miranda went on. "From what I've read, the site to the north is federal land that's being granted to them. But if they get the right senators or congress members and the governor to go along with cutting funds for the state park, they might not grant it, but they can justify selling this area. Orchids would be the only thing left standing in their way."

"They couldn't take the park without setting off mass protests," said Jack.

"Once the sale of the park becomes law and is legal and finally made public, all they need to do is send in the police to protect the purchase against protestors," said Miranda. "That's you, Jack."

Doris was the first to notice a vehicle creeping down the driveway toward the house. It was a black SUV, and it was slowly approaching as though the occupants were scoping out the land.

"I need to install a gate," said Doris.

Miranda and Jack simultaneously turned to peer through the kitchen windows where Doris was looking. Miranda nearly knocked the chair over as she went to the window and brushed aside the lace curtain to get a better view. "Do you recognize it?"

"No," said Doris. "It's too new looking for anyone around here. "

Miranda nudged Jack aside and quickly returned to the table, where she began pacing.

"If it's the killer, what is he doing here?" she said. "Why would he come back?"

"Maybe we're overreacting. It's probably someone from out of town wanting the land," said Doris. "I'll send them away."

"Stay in the house, Doris."

Miranda attached the photo to a text message titled "facial recognition this," touched the "Send" button, and hoped that Blake, her supervisor, received it and that he'd be able to identify the man.

"I hate it when we're right," she said. "Remind me to apologize for all the grief I caused my aunt Rita. She wanted to keep me on the beach with her, which in hindsight was smart."

CHAPTER
Seven

BAD GUYS IN BLACK SUVS

Miranda turned away from the window after she took a picture of the license plate.

"It could be the guy in the photo," said Jack.

"But why would he come back to the scene?" Miranda asked. "And if he is the guy in the photo, I don't want to arrest him and bring him in until we get wiretap clearance. If we alert anyone that we have him, everyone will become tight-lipped, and there goes our chance of trapping Ethan Richards."

Jack asked Miranda if she wanted him to try calling for backup.

Miranda's pacing across the kitchen floor intensified.

"We can't call your department for backup," she said. "We have to protect what we have so no one gets wind of it. And right now, there aren't a lot of people I trust."

For a moment, she thought of taking the photo they'd gotten from Doris's camera and ending the case right there. These people would be happy turning in one of their own as long as Ethan Richards wasn't implicated and the company was left intact. Then she also thought back to yesterday and working in the Twin

Cities, risking her life to push things as far as needed and never feeling appreciated for it. But being with Jack and Doris reminded her that she hadn't joined the FBI to feel appreciated.

She tapped her teeth with her finger and thought. And then the answer of escape came to her.

"Jack, how good are you with a rifle?" Miranda asked. "You want me to shoot them?"

"I should have been more prepared and had an exit strategy," said Miranda. "But I really wasn't sure we'd find anything so damning, and it's just my luck that we would." She looked directly at Jack.

"Take Doris's rifle and go out the back and work your way around to the front, so if this goes bad, we have a backup. Don't let them see you."

Doris reached into her pocket, took out a handful of bullets, and gave them to Jack. "You're asking me to cover you?"

"This could be their attempt to get rid of any witnesses. And with this photo, we have a glimmer of hope of gaining some assistance, and I don't want to lose it," said Miranda. "If you see anything that doesn't look right, send a message by taking out a mirror or a headlight to let them know you're there. If that doesn't work and they attack us, then you may have to shoot them to defend us."

"You're serious?" said Jack. "I'm not part of the FBI sniper force."

"No, but I've tried telling you the circumstances of this case aren't normal. Try not to kill anyone if you can help it, but I've been warning you about this all morning. If you care about getting everyone involved in David Willis's murder, we have to prevent them from knowing what we have. They're forcing our hand."

Miranda touched Doris on the shoulder and looked her in the eyes while speaking to Jack.

"If something doesn't seem right, Doris and I will go out the front and get in my car. That's your signal to pay attention. At the end of the driveway, we'll turn left. When you're finished distracting them, circle back to the road, and we'll pick you up there."

"An orchestrated getaway is somehow better than calling the police?" said Jack.

"You are the police. And there's a reason why I don't have plates on my car. I know it's among the thousand questions you've wanted to ask. It's in case we need to protect our lives and the integrity of the case by keeping them guessing."

Doris handed Jack the rifle. "It's an inch low at two hundred yards," she said.

"What about windage?"

"It's on," said Doris. "And if it's not, there's no time now to fix it."

"Go, Jack," said Miranda. "They could have dropped some-one off farther up the driveway, so watch yourself."

Jack felt like he was being rushed off to protect against an invading army, one he couldn't see with clear markings but one that seemed real based on what he'd seen on David Willis's forehead and from what he'd heard from Ethan Richards manipulating David's grieving mother. He didn't like the feeling of helplessness or responsibility, but it was clear at that moment no one was coming to bail them out.

He lifted his head and with gun in hand rushed out the back door.

Miranda closed her eyes, wishing she could stop time, if only for twenty seconds more. Maybe all of this was nothing. Maybe it was like Doris had said, and they only wanted to ask about buying the land. But she sensed that wasn't the case.

When the SUV came to a stop, the first man stepped out of the driver's side and surveyed the property and the horizon in all directions. Then he looked at Miranda's government-issued Camry and then at the house.

From inside the kitchen where Miranda and Doris were standing, the man's hair looked brown, cut short like the guy in the photo, but it likely wasn't the shooter. He closed the car door and adjusted the gun holster he wore over his black T-shirt. Miranda couldn't tell for sure what kind of pistol he had because the SUV was blocking her view. It wasn't illegal for him to have a gun because of the newly-passed concealed carry laws, and EPA agents carried weapons. However, her gut still told her this vehicle and this guy had nothing to do with any law-abiding governmental agency that protected the environment or wildlife.

The second man climbed out of the passenger side, which was closest to the house. He closed the door, looked at the black Camry, and noticed it didn't have license plates. He then looked at the barn to the right and at the UTV parked in front of the house. He wore camo pants and a black compression shirt, and his upper body wasn't as built as the other guy's. He didn't appear to have a gun. But it was his air of confidence and the arrogance radiating from his stiff posture and gelled hair that made Miranda believe he was the one in control. But he also wasn't the shooter in the photo.

A tree line was in front of the house to the east, two hundred fifty yards away. Miranda knew it was a long way even for a trained FBI sniper to shoot, but it was the only good cover offering them an open and clear shot at the men.

Jack, if ever there was a time to step up and believe me and everything we've talked about, it's now, Miranda thought.

"Put the book with the orchid in it away," she said to Doris. "And follow me and be ready to lock up behind us. We have to be ready to move, and we can't let them know what we have, so let me do the talking."

Doris wrapped the book in her arms and held it tightly to her body like it was something cherished from long ago, like a present someone had given her, and put it away. Then she came back to the door with her keys in hand.

Before the man reached the front steps, Miranda opened the door and stood in the entryway, blocking it. She had her hand inside her jacket, and she slowly ran her fingers across the ridges on the grip of her gun. She knew her gun like she knew what it felt like to stand on a surfboard or the weight of her reading glasses resting on her head.

"Stop where you are," she said to the man.

She'd said it loudly enough that the driver looked over. But the man she was talking to scanned the ground before him as he

continued walking toward the steps. He pretended to be preoccupied with the dull ground as he kept approaching. His eyes had
no vibrant color to them.

This time Miranda didn't hesitate to pull her pistol into view.

"I said stop. I'm not asking you again," she said. She said it
softly and with a tone of indifference that emphasized she was
serious.

The man stopped abruptly and looked up at her.

"Who are you?" said Miranda.

Impressed by the beautiful figure before him, the man took a
second to regain his composure.

"I'm with Global Econ Mining."

"Why are you here?" asked Miranda.

"Why do you have your gun out when a vehicle pulls up?" the
man asked.

Miranda understood it as a question to disarm or give away
her identity. She'd been in enough of these situations not to be
fooled anymore.

"My mother heard someone was killed in the park," she said.
"So she called me. I'm here looking out for her."

The man squatted to pick up a small stone and then stood
again. He appeared agitated that he had to continue this conversation with her. Her intriguing beauty had lost its appeal.

"As I was saying, we're with Global Econ Mining. The man
killed was working for us."

"David Willis. A biologist. I read about it in the paper," said
Miranda.

"Then you know the full story."

"We know the story the paper printed, but these days people
create their own stories to lead people away from the truth, so
I question how accurate the small-town reporting is, just like I
question you telling me who David Willis was working for. The
papers also said something about an environmentalist being
behind the killing. But I have a difficult time believing an environmentalist would kill a biologist. It seems to me they'd be on the
same team, so I'm wondering if the newspapers aren't being paid
to lie about what really happened to conceal the truth."

The man looked back at the driver and then stared directly at Miranda. He seemed to be listening intently to the conversation, assessing his next course of action.

"The way you hold that gun suggests you've held one before," said the man. "Do you always carry a gun?"

"Lately I have to because of all of the violence," said Miranda. Then she motioned to the driver. "You guys carry too?"

"We sometimes come across radicals we have to deal with to protect ourselves and our interests."

"I've often had to deal with radicals and protect my interests as well," said Miranda. "And right now, my mother's safety is my interest."

"We'd like to ask her some questions about whether or not she saw anything yesterday. We're going around asking everyone what they saw and what their knowledge of the area is. We're doing some follow-up investigating."

The man took a step toward Miranda.

"Not another step," she said.

The man froze before he lifted his foot and could put it down again.

Miranda moved from the front door out onto the porch.

"Lock the door behind you, Doris, and hold onto me if you have to."

The man moved toward them as Doris fumbled with the lock, thinking Miranda was distracted. This time Miranda raised her gun and pointed it at his head.

"Animals are trained to listen better than you are," said Miranda. "Tell me why you're really here, and tell your guy to drop his gun."

"We're well within our rights to be here."

Doris tightly clutched the back of Miranda's coat to help her balance.

"I don't know what world you think you live in," said Miranda. "But your rights do not include coming here onto this property, threatening us, and acting like you own us or this place. Tell your guy to drop his gun, back away to give us room to come down these steps, and if you refuse, I will see that as a threat."

The driver, who still stood next to the SUV, made a casual but defiant move for his gun. When he did, and without warning, the side mirror next to him exploded into shrapnel. The echoing boom of the gun shot was heard a second later.

The driver lost hold of his gun as he shielded his eyes and face from the shattered glass and plastic. When he regained his bearing, he looked toward the tree line where he thought he'd heard the shot.

The other man, the one closest to Miranda and Doris, had blinked his eyes and flinched, although he didn't appear terribly rattled by the shot.

Derrick?" the driver called to the man closest to Miranda, suggesting to Derrick that if they were going to do something, they'd better do it now.

But Derrick didn't say a word. Instead, he put out his hand to the driver as though to quiet him and to suggest everything was going to be fine.

"Derrick," said Miranda. "That must be the rogue environmentalist that has everyone so worried."

Derrick slowly shook his head as he motioned for the driver to leave his gun on the ground where it had fallen.

Miranda wondered again how many others were hiding behind tinted windows in the SUV. She had to trust in Jack; if anyone emerged, he'd take care of them. Her focus had to remain on Doris and on the man named Derrick.

"Doris, reach into my pocket and grab the keys. And you," she said to Derrick, "Move to the other side of the car in the line of fire with your friend."

Derrick hesitated for a moment, but he moved before she had to ask him twice.

"When you can hear the whistle of the bullet hit its target before the report of the gun, it suggests someone's been trained," said Derrick.

"If that's true, I feel lucky to have such a talented environmentalist looking out for us."

Miranda led Doris safely around the SUV to her Camry and into the driver's seat. Then she closed the door for Doris, came around the back side of the car toward the passenger door, and kept her gun on the men.

The men gave her a wide berth.

"Firing on someone without displaying a badge is breaking the law," said Derrick.

"You're talking to me about breaking the law? If it takes someone shooting at you to care about honesty and false pretenses, you should be shot at more often. You're lucky that person out there is giving you a second chance at life. You might not be so lucky next time."

Miranda ducked her head inside the car and took her eyes off the men, and Derrick took a step toward them. When he did, the dirt next to him exploded. Again the late report of the shot echoed like an explosion from a cannon hidden somewhere in the distant tree line. Derrick instinctively raised his hand to shield his eyes from the fragments of grass and dirt.

Jack breathed in, held it once more, and slowly squeezed the trigger again. This time he took out one of the SUV's front tires. The vehicle dropped as though the ground had fallen out from underneath it.

Miranda put her gun in her lap as Doris started the car and drove them away. When they got farther down the driveway, she leaned over and hugged Doris.

"We'll send someone out to look after the place, so I don't want you to worry."

Doris looked straight ahead and gripped the steering wheel.

"If you and Jack hadn't been here, they would have killed me," said Doris.

"I don't know why they were here," said Miranda.

"You don't have to sugarcoat this for me. We'd be dead if Jack hadn't stopped them."

"Yes," Miranda confessed. "They might have killed us. But Jack came through, didn't he? And it would be nice to know who this Derrick character is. We should switch places up ahead."

When they were out of view of the SUV, Doris stopped the car. Miranda took Doris gently by the arm and helped her around the front to the passenger side and buckled her in. Then

Miranda, back behind the wheel, turned left onto the paved road like she'd told Jack she would and dialed 911.

She told the dispatcher to send someone out to Doris Lewis's house to deal with mining company trespassers who were armed and dangerous. The dispatcher asked if there was a standoff. Miranda said two men threatened Doris Lewis and that whoever came should arrive in tactical gear. She didn't know the police chief's number (if she remembered from talking with Jack, his name was Steve) to speak directly with him. She trusted they'd handle it.

They drove for a quarter mile before pulling over at the side of the road.

"Now what do we do?" said Doris.

"We'll need to find you a place to stay temporarily until we get someone out here to watch over you at your place," Miranda conceded. She felt terrible telling her she'd just been evicted from her home.

"I was lucky you were both here," said Doris.

"I don't know if they were there for you or us, so maybe we're all lucky."

When Jack saw Miranda and Doris, he ran out of the woods and up onto the road. He slumped over and rested his hands on his knees as he tried to catch his breath. He couldn't remember the last time he'd run so fast. He had Doris's rifle slung over his shoulder. He caught his breath and trotted toward the car. Miranda pulled ahead to meet him halfway.

"Did they see you? Are they behind you?" she asked.

Miranda scanned the woods near the road's edge.

Jack, still gasping for air, shook his head. Then he opened the door, laid the gun gently on the seat so he wouldn't jar the scope, and flung himself inside on the floor of the backseat.

"I should have never doubted you," said Jack.

Jack didn't have the door closed before Miranda pressed the accelerator to the floor.

"They had this planned all along," said Miranda. "They researched an environmentalist in the area and sent the goon in the photo to steal the weapon to use it to silence David Willis.

But they must have felt they overlooked something to return to the crime scene, or they heard about you and me, Jack, and they caught up with us."

"They were making sure there were no witnesses," said Doris.

"Maybe. Or they're trying to silence anyone who might have knowledge of orchids."

"I got a text from Bill saying they're holding Trenton Fuller on murder charges," said Jack. "It doesn't make sense."

When Jack said it, and now that the three of them were safe in the car, Miranda's instinct was to keep driving toward the coast. But she was with two competent people now who felt as strongly about solving this case as she did. And they had a picture of the killer.

"If you think you can trust your department with the photo to get Trenton out of trouble, give it to them, but not unless you have to," said Miranda. "I'll get a request for wiretaps and phone records sent in, but this plan to catch them talking openly about any involvement is sure to fail if word is leaked that we have a photo of the killer, so be careful about who you tell."

"I've known Steve my whole life," said Jack. "And I have no idea what he's thinking by holding Trenton on murder charges. I'd better get over there and get it cleared up."

"Doris and I already called to have someone from your department sent to her place," said Miranda. "We're going to the Ramada Inn to get rooms, so meet us there. Plus, I'll try and get the iCloud password from David Willis's fiancé. If his phone no longer exists, and if he did photograph anything, I'm hoping he was able to send it out."

"I wish I would have grabbed some of my belongings," said Doris.

Miranda saw the hurt on Doris's face at being driven from her home.

"Doris," said Jack, "can you show us on a map where you used to see orchids?"

"I know a place where I used to find them by the hundreds, but it's not an easy hike."

Doris's complexion and eyes weren't as vibrant as when Jack

and Miranda had first met her.

"This is about to get heated because now they know we're onto them. Jack, I'll take you to the park to get your truck, and then you do what you can to break Trenton out of jail. While you're doing that, I'll do what I can to find a connection between the killer in the photo and Ethan Richards. And then I'll try to motivate someone in my department to care enough to help us understand why so many people are determined to keep the truth behind David Willis's murder a secret."

CHAPTER
Eight
THE RESCUE

Jack stood before his supervisor in a small office filled with baseball trophies and plaques. The desk was tidy. A laptop in the center had MLB stats pulled up on the screen, with pens and sticky notes lying orderly next to it.

"When I told Bill to have Trenton Fuller brought in, I didn't say to have him brought in for questioning," said Jack.

Steve was short and stocky and five years younger than Jack. That Steve had passed him up the department ladder didn't bother Jack. Jack was never one to play the games needed to become a department head. Steve had also been a local sports hero, taking the baseball team to state, where they'd gotten second place, giving him a boost of recognition. He'd surrounded himself with the trophies he'd won from middle school to high school. Being a good athlete was an important attribute in Clearwater that typically elevated people's status. Even though Jack's son played sports, Jack didn't always like how the focus on athleticism took away from the attention on academic fortitude and success.

"Bill said you called to have Trenton Fuller brought in, and that's what we did," said Steve.

"I told him he's a target and to protect him," Jack clarified. "So, where was the breakdown in communication?"

"You said he had the gun that matched the murder weapon."

"I said he might have a gun that matched the murder weapon but that we don't think he's the killer."

"What do you have proving that he didn't do it?" asked Steve.

Jack stared at his supervisor for a moment, wondering if this was a joke being played on him.

"Other than the fact that we don't even have the gun, so we have no way to match ballistics?" said Jack. "And you want to hold him on murder charges? Are you kidding? You're manufacturing a case for a fake arrest warrant."

"He has a 270 rifle registered to him."

"So do a thousand other people in this area, Steve. So by your logic, doesn't that mean we should be bringing all of them in and arresting them too?"

"You're the one who narrowed it down to Trenton."

"Because someone's been spreading lies, saying an environmentalist killed David Willis, and it's not true. Are you in on this with them?"

"What are you talking about?"

Jack thought of trying to explain how he had also been given Trenton's name from David Willis's mother, which had been given to her by the likely killer in an attempt to set him up, but he worried it would only confuse Steve and implicate Trenton even more.

"Trenton speaks out," said Jack, "and he's local, so we suspect he's being set up to silence him and cover the murder while fueling support for Global Econ Mining. It's a campaign to smear him. Someone is using propaganda to confuse everyone, and obviously, it's working."

"I look at the facts, and all you've been doing is riding around all morning with this FBI agent none of us have met yet, so making the connection that Trenton is the one who did it is more than you've produced."

Jack started to speak but immediately stopped himself. He remembered how Miranda had tried getting through to Diane that morning and how easy it'd be to walk out the door. But he understood the need to try and make Steve understand what was happening to the community. Any support Jack received from Steve, including freeing an innocent man from jail, depended on how well he explained the situation.

"We suspect *The Chronicle* and another paper are providing the lies with the hope of setting up someone like Trenton. We know this because it looks like Jeff purposely changed the statement I gave him yesterday to hide the identity of the real killer. We also spoke with David Willis's mother, who confirmed that the mining company is putting out a false story. They wouldn't do that unless they were trying to cover for it and spin all of us in circles, which is working because you're defending them and playing along by holding Trenton."

Steve rose from his chair and began to pace, giving himself time to consider what Jack was trying to tell him. He rubbed his chin as he thought.

"Why would Jeff Harvey get himself involved in a murder?"

"I don't think he's involved in the killing but probably in the cover-up. He probably needs the money."

"Jeff wouldn't spread lies to protect a killer."

"I didn't want to believe it either, but it looks like that's exactly what he's doing."

"What did Jeff say when you confronted him?"

"I haven't spoken with him yet. We were unable to reach him. But we talked with Diane, and she denied misrepresenting what I'd said, which is a lie. That or she simply doesn't know."

"Or there's nothing there," said Steve. He sat again, leaned back in his leather seat, and folded his arms.

Steve was refusing to hear that Jeff Harvey could be involved in covering for a murder, but the fact that he wasn't yelling made Jack think maybe he was getting through to him.

"Accusing a mining company like Global Econ Mining of killing someone is not something to take lightly," said Steve. "And have you read the papers? They could bring jobs to this area."

"I keep hearing that, but no one ever questions at what cost, or how many jobs, or if it's even true," said Jack.

"Why do you think they'd do something like kill David Willis?"

"Because he was about to reveal something. We suspect David Willis found something that could threaten the mining operation's plans, so they had him killed, and the company is using the media to cover it," said Jack.

He could feel his blood pressure rising.

"Trenton Fuller is being implicated based on rumors and lies about something he didn't do."

"You and this agent have proof this mining company is involved and would do something like this?"

Jack remembered what Miranda had told him about being cautious with information.

"We have a man, Ethan Richards, who works for the mining company, asking David Willis's mother to release her son's name in the newspaper ahead of our investigation."

"What's the significance of that?"

"Why would they be asking to release the name of someone who was killed who didn't even work for them?" said Jack. "And before anyone else even knew he'd been killed? Don't be fooled by the spin they're putting out there to hide what they've done."

"Did you call Ethan Richards?"

"He's on the list of stops, but I had to come here first because I need to take care of Trenton Fuller."

"A lot of people tell me you're wrong about Trenton."

"Because they're full of hate, and they're blind. Either they're part of the organization involved, or they're too confused by the lies to see Trenton is harmless, and they're only looking out for themselves."

Before Steve could respond, Jack took out his phone and hit the record button. He wanted to document the narrative in case he ever needed it.

He cleared his throat and began the story that was already getting old for him. It was then that he realized how much he appreciated Doris and Miranda, who didn't need details.

"...I think this Ethan Richards wanted to have David Willis killed, so someone working for him did their research, broke in and stole Trenton's gun, killed David Willis with it, and they're setting up Trenton to make him look like the killer. But you know Trenton. He's a victim who needs protecting. He can be abrasive and opinionated about certain topics, but he's not a killer."

When Jack finished, he hit the red "stop" button.

"In my mind, we have enough to hold him," said Steve.

Jack felt like he was talking to a child, which gave him another idea.

"You try not to let your opponent outsmart you in baseball, and it's the same with this. You're manufacturing a guilty verdict of an innocent person based on what the other team is telling you to trick you into letting them win. And it's working because you believe Trenton is guilty when there's no real evidence to support it. Don't play the game these criminals want us to play."

"Then give me something definitive that can clear him."

"Besides the fact that we're being stupid right now talking about how he might be guilty and that I wanted him brought in to protect him, not prosecute him? We don't even have the murder weapon."

Jack glared as Steve leaned forward again. If Steve was so thick as not to understand what he was telling him, the honest thing to do was to tell him they had a photo of the killer, who most likely was carrying Trenton Fuller's gun with a homemade silencer on it. But he agreed with Miranda that they couldn't risk word getting out.

"The evidence you're forming against him is based on lies," Jack continued. "It's what this Ethan Richards does to get away with taking whatever property he wants to take. But look at the facts. All we know is that a 270 killed David Willis, and Trenton had one. But a million other people around here also own them, and you know that."

"But his gun is conveniently missing," said Steve. "If he's innocent, why didn't he ever report his gun as stolen or missing?"

"You and I both have guns at home that we never regularly

inventory that someone could sneak into our homes and take to frame us," said Jack. "Don't help them by making up stories."

Steve folded his arms and leaned back in his chair.

Jack, hoping the pause in the conversation was long enough for Steve to catch on that he was holding an innocent man, put his hands in his pockets to diffuse the situation. He thought a few seconds would be long enough for his supervisor to come to his senses.

"These people are professionals at driving wedges between people like you and me in communities like ours so they can get what they want. This is bigger than a local environmentalist taking out his hate on someone like the papers are reporting," Jack said. "Now is the time when we have to come together so we can figure out what these people are really after."

"I granted you permission to call the FBI because I trusted you to come up with something more than speculation," said Steve. "But right now, Trenton Fuller seems to be the only solid thing we're sitting on."

"It's not him. Miranda thinks, and I agree with her, that there's an orchid in the valley that the EPA and The Nature Conservancy overlooked. She thinks this mining company wants to mine the state park."

"Christ," said Steve. "For copper?"

He shook his head and leaned over his hands on his desk.

"It's more than possible," said Jack.

"So is the possibility of being run out of here for following crazy conspiracies."

"Locking up an innocent man with no evidence is following and practicing conspiracy. And if we present the people with the truth and they crucify us for it, then we really have become a third-world country. So if no one will listen to reality, maybe it is time to pack up and start over somewhere else. It's a state park now. But if you watch the news, there's been talk about cutting funding for the parks. The next legislature could make it viable to sell it if they make the argument that caring for it costs too much."

"Now who's reaching? Your FBI woman friend got you to

believe that?"

Jack briefly went into the specific history of the mining company and what Miranda had said they'd been recorded doing in South America, but Steve began zoning out. South America was another planet to Steve. Jack realized he had to try a different approach that would resonate with him.

"Doris Lewis said orchids used to grow in the valley years ago. We think the mining company had David Willis killed because he found an orchid on the endangered list that will prevent them from coming into the area."

"Dispatch received a call from a government number to send someone out to the old Lewis place, not far from where the body was found, something about threats being made, but when officers got there, they found nothing. Sometime before that, the guys finishing up in the park swore they heard shooting. Do you know anything about it?"

Sweat formed on Jack's lip. He hoped his whiskers were thick enough to hide it.

"The government number must be Miranda's."

"What were you two doing at the Lewis place?"

"Asking Mrs. Lewis if she'd seen anything suspicious."

"Had she?"

"No."

"And then what happened?"

Jack's mind started drifting as he thought of walking out of the office to go see Miranda at the Ramada Inn. Then he swallowed, knowing he was going to stay where he was and that he was always a terrible liar.

Jack told him a cover story about wanting to go into the park from Doris's property but that he'd gotten lost and ended up on the road where Miranda and Doris saw him and picked him up. He was impressed with himself for rattling it off so quickly.

"Why'd this FBI agent have Mrs. Lewis with her?"

"To protect her from some guys who pulled up. You can ask her when you see her, which reminds me that I have to get moving, so let me have Trenton so we can continue going after the real killers."

Steve slid his chair back and stood. He ran his hand over the back of his neck and walked around in the little office space he had. He picked up a baseball bat and gripped it as though he were reminiscing about the last time he was up to the plate ten years ago.

"Trenton Fuller is innocent, and to think he's guilty of murder is crazy," Jack reiterated.

"A lot of people would have issues with letting him go."

"And it's good they're not in charge of making these decisions, or they'd have many more of the falsely accused locked up."

Jack was optimistic that a sliver of logic was making its way through.

"What if it turns out to be nothing, and what if everyone else is right about Trenton Fuller being the killer?"

"It's time to stop listening to certain people in the community," said Jack. "It's our job to be better and protect people being slandered."

"Why doesn't the FBI just take over the case?"

"I don't know the full story, but I get the feeling the FBI is struggling with help."

"Probably because they're all a bunch of educated assholes, and no one wants to work for them anymore. But it might be good to have both of your asses put in a sling. If I give you Trenton Fuller—and I know this is stupid—anything he does is on you."

"Of course."

"If he fucks up and goes on a killing rampage, that'll be on you. But I also can't be responsible for a company like this moving into our area if they really are a bunch of killers and thieves. Then we all lose."

"That's smart."

"Don't you talk down to me! I'll give you and this FBI agent two days to prove Trenton's not guilty. After that, unless I hear the FBI has taken over the case and stops fucking us by only assisting us, you're bringing him back in. And you'll be sitting in a jail cell with him for being an idiot."

CHAPTER
Nine

FORMING ALLIANCES

This jailhouse is like an asylum run by the people who should be committed, thought Trenton Fuller as he stepped up and into Jack's police truck. He situated himself on the seat and then placed his worn and faded mustard-yellow Nature Conservancy hat on his head. He closed the door behind himself. He didn't think it latched, so he opened it and slammed it to be sure.

Jack was already buckled in and starting the engine.

"I told Bill Winslow to have you brought in for your protection because I know he's someone I can trust, but the others didn't listen. It feels like my fault, but somehow communication broke down, but I was trying to help you. It's like Steve's brain, and some of the others', has turned to mush overnight," said Jack.

"I don't think the decay has been that sudden," said Trenton.

Being part of the police force, Jack didn't know if he should nod in agreement even though he wanted to.

"I've seen your name in the papers before. Your name is Jack

Calaway. Is that right?" Trenton asked as he looked at the highway and readjusted the bill of his cap.

"Yes. And I can't believe the breakdown in logic that's been happening," said Jack. "Somehow, they heard the word prosecute instead of protect when they brought you in."

"The officers in your department kept asking me about the gun and why someone like me would own one. Hunting wasn't a good enough answer, even though 90 percent of the people around here hunt or have guns. After reading last night that a biologist was killed in the park, I figured everything out. I didn't murder anyone. But they wouldn't even hear what I had to say."

"It's because their minds have gone numb from all of the mining propaganda. Or they're purposely choosing to side against you and label you a killer because they support the mining operation, which is worse. I was warned about the effect all fake news stories could have on people over time, but I didn't want to believe it could be so bad that it could alter people's logic. It's taken us off track."

Trenton, being the concerned environmentalist he was, was well informed about the history of the mining company, its manipulative tactics, and the destruction it left behind in places like South America. When Jack acknowledged the existence of the department's bias, a realization that startled Jack himself, Trenton's spirit seemed to lift a bit. But Trenton didn't know if he could completely trust Jack. The department had let him down countless times whenever his house or car was vandalized.

"You understand how this works," said Trenton. "You know about the mining company's involvement?"

"We don't know their entire game, but we're slowly piecing it together and learning who's involved."

Jack wanted to tell Trenton about the photo of the guy carrying what was most likely his rifle, but he couldn't risk giving out specific information. He was still optimistic that Miranda was having luck linking the killer to Ethan Richards and getting wiretaps.

And Jack was impressed by Trenton's knowledge and insight about what seemed more and more likely to be happening in the community. He could see Trenton becoming a valuable asset in the fight to expose them.

"Why are you the only one in the police force who can figure any of this out?"

"I've been working with a good FBI agent who takes the time to explain how they're doing it. Everything she's said has been right and makes sense based on what I've seen."

Jack took a moment to reflect on everything he'd observed: David Willis's defaced body, the blundered discussions with Diane and Steve, David Willis's traumatized and grieving mother, Trenton being framed, and Miranda—wonderful Miranda. He was fully aware that had he not fired on the SUV at Doris's place, something awful most likely would have happened to Doris or Miranda. It was a turning point for him in accepting everything Miranda had tried explaining earlier.

"For a civilian and someone who's gotten dragged into this, you're quick to understand the plot against you," said Jack.

"When you're constantly victimized, you catch on quickly to the games a big corporation like this plays," said Trenton. "You might think I'm crazy, but I think they're after the state park. So they kill a biologist for whatever reason and blame it on an environmentalist like me, and that only fuels the locals' hatred for anyone challenging the mining company. And I don't think I'm crazy because the legislature is already discussing cutting park funding. If that passes, the next step would be to understaff the park and let it fall into disrepair, so they can justify to the voters the need to sell it. They have think tanks that dream this crap up."

Jack thought back to the morning and how he'd questioned Miranda about some of her speculative comments. After all that he'd seen that morning, and as he sat listening to Trenton, he didn't find them bizarre anymore.

"We agree that they're most likely after the state park, but how do we prove it to let the people of Clearwater in on it?" Jack said.

"I don't know if that's ever possible."

Trenton adjusted his round, wire-framed glasses.

"But it doesn't matter what any of us suspect because we're powerless without police protection and the power of the courts to help piece it all together and prosecute them," said Trenton.

"If we were powerless, they wouldn't be trying so hard to keep us quiet. I'm learning too that stepping up and standing out puts a target on your back."

"Why are you wearing a target?" asked Trenton.

"Because I defended you for doing nothing wrong. And as far as I'm concerned, you're free to go," said Jack. "It's already been proven you're innocent, but we can't tell anyone yet, and I can't tell you how I know, but based on what we found, even the most ignorant DA would have to toss out a case against you."

"Whatever evidence you have won't be good enough," said Trenton. "Once you release me, even if you can prove I'm innocent, the attacks will be back because I've been branded a killer of progress and now a people killer. Nothing I say or do will change the viewpoint of people like Steve."

Having spoken with Diane and now Steve, who refused to listen to any reasoning, Jack was beginning to see the truth in Trenton's statement.

"It does feel like sides have been formed, and our community is being ripped apart by lies. And somehow, I missed how people were feeling and that someone had been working on creating division in our community. Things like that don't happen in a day, but this murder has certainly brought it to light. Stay with us and help us show people the truth by solving this murder," said Jack.

"Maybe the people you want to show the truth to already know what the truth is. Have you ever thought of that?"

"Not until recently, but I think there are enough people not involved who still want us looking out for them."

"I'm not law enforcement. So how am I supposed to help? And stay with whom?"

"Miranda and me."

"Who's Miranda?"

"The FBI agent leading the case. She's young but sharp. I want you to help us locate a plant in the state park," said Jack. "Do you know Mrs. Lewis?"

"I know of Doris Lewis," said Trenton. "Why?"

"Doris suggested we look for orchids, that maybe there's an endangered species in the park that could be standing in the way of this mining operation, and maybe David Willis was going to report it. So they had him killed."

Trenton placed both his hands beside himself on the seat. He slowly, methodically breathed in and out to keep from overreacting.

"Doris Lewis told you that?"

"Yes."

"Is she an expert on orchids?"

"Not that I know of, but she knows of them."

"Then why the hell would you get an old woman mixed up in something like this?"

"I didn't. Two guys claiming to be from the mining company drove out to her place asking what she'd seen."

"Why do they care what she'd seen unless she saw something or knows something they don't want her to?"

Jack sat quietly for a second so Trenton could hear his own words.

"Now you understand the threats and intimidation tactics are being directed on a larger scale, and not only toward you," said Jack.

Trenton nodded his head slowly. He seemed even more concerned now as if he were connecting all the pieces.

"We were out there taking care of a situation when I got word that they were holding you," said Jack. "So it's not just you or me impacted by this."

"Where is Doris now?"

"She's with Miranda."

Trenton breathed another sigh of resignation.

"These people have probably been planning for months to coordinate the media and to create a plan to frame an environmentalist," said Jack. "And I didn't want to believe it, but it seems more likely that they killed David Willis to hide something that's going to be detrimental to this area. You can help clear yourself among the community by helping us figure out what it is."

"How can I ever change the hatred these people feel for me?" Trenton asked. "I have a degree in environmental biology. I used to inspect in-ground fuel tank removals. Now I work occasionally as a consultant. I'm like a foreign spy to most of the people around here."

"Are you familiar with rare plant species in the area?"

"Some."

"Could David Willis have found an endangered orchid in the boundaries of the state park?"

The hardened lines on Trenton's face softened.

"Orchids that would fall under the environmental protection laws are extremely rare, and usually that type of thing is already documented."

"If they can't change the environmental protection laws, maybe the mining company is trying to pressure someone to declare the orchids are no longer here when they know they are. Have you ever come across any?"

"No, but I haven't been looking for them either. But even if this biologist did find some, why kill him in the park where someone would find him? And how'd they know where he was unless they were with him or tailing him?"

"I don't have all the answers, but Miranda thinks that the company was pressuring David Willis to give some sort of legal clearance for the company to access the land in this area, and he didn't conform to what they were asking."

Trenton readjusted his glasses. It was as though he were trapped within a firestorm of information, burning the last of his hope that the situation wasn't as bad as it seemed.

"I always suspected this area would become a target for mining copper on a commercial scale," he said. "It's probably inevitable. But killing for it shows you the kind of destruction these people will bring and what they'll do to the community and diversity if they gain a foothold here."

Jack lowered the window to get air on his tired face. He pulled his phone from his pocket and checked his text messages.

Trenton watched the road and was ready to grab the wheel if needed.

"And not only do I have to worry about the public like you getting sucked into this mess, now I have to worry about my son. I met some of these mining people. They seem like the type who have no issue wrecking lives to get what they want," said Jack.

"They framed me, and now your captain wants to charge me with murder, so I can attest to them wrecking lives. Where is your son?"

"He should be at tennis practice by now. School is just about to finish up."

Even though Trenton had just been freed from jail, he questioned whether these people would threaten someone's child. Then he looked at Jack's tired face, at his holstered pistol, and at the door of the county-issued vehicle in which he was currently riding in. Trenton felt lucky that he hadn't been killed.

"You're probably questioning whether or not to take on these people. It'd be easy to leave and let them have the entire area," said Trenton.

"It's probably a smart move, but I've seen the bad guys, and I don't want them taking my town."

"I'm beginning to wonder if I should move somewhere less violent and vulnerable and forget about what happens here," said Trenton. "But it's my home, and I can't let go of it either."

Jack remembered how concerned Miranda appeared when he'd first met her at the chateau. When he thought of what he'd done at Doris's and what he'd had to say to Steve, he saw flashes of the white sandy beaches Miranda had shown him. And hearing the suggestion from Trenton about how practical it would be to leave made him feel sick. Had he been the only one who didn't already realize that his community had been "bought" and overrun by the influence of the mining company?

"If we don't leave now, we'll probably need an exit strategy in case things get even more heated," said Trenton.

"I've already had this conversation with Miranda," said Jack.

"If it turns out that these people are behind both the murder and my missing gun, and if nothing is done to them because of the money they have, then we have to begin questioning if what we're doing is worth it," said Trenton. "But until we figure out exactly how much trouble we're in, I'll do what I can to help. It will take more than you, and obviously, your department has no idea what they're doing."

At the tennis courts, Jack remembered his conversation with Trenton as he hung one hand onto the woven wire fence at the far end. He had chosen a corner far from the aluminum bleachers where a few high school kids sat scattered, watching the practice.

"Aiden," Jack called loud enough for his son to hear.

Aiden looked over at his dad, then at his coach, who was working with some freshmen. Jacob, his doubles partner, was on the other court talking with some girls through the fence. Aiden jogged through the narrow opening in the fence and outside the tennis courts and over to see his dad.

"I texted a while ago," said Jack as his son slowed to a walk. "Why didn't you text me back?"

"I got busy. I figured it could wait."

"I don't want you ignoring my texts. I was worried."

"If you came here to yell at me, then get the hell away from me."

Aiden turned around.

"You're the one yelling," said Jack. "You need to learn to control your anger, and just because your mom rips on me doesn't give you that right. I'm here because there was a murder in the state park yesterday afternoon."

Aiden stopped his defiant walk back to the safety of the tennis courts and turned to face his dad.

"I heard," he said. "Everyone has been talking about it. They're saying some dumbass environmentalist went nuts."

Then Aiden noticed someone was sitting in the front seat of his dad's police truck. He lifted his head to look over the top of his dad so he could get a better look.

"Is that one of the suspects?"

"It's Trenton Fuller."

"Trenton Fuller? Isn't he the guy who has a website page and is always going on about the environment?"

"Yes."

"Is it him?"

"No. And don't believe the garbage people are circulating. You have to be strong and stand against it, or you could become a target too. He's not a suspect. He's working with me on this murder investigation. And I think you should pack up and come with us."

"Why would I come with you? I just started practice." Aiden looked over his shoulder at his teammates before turning back to his dad.

"Because there are people here who might hurt us, and I don't want anything to happen to you. This is beyond what Mom can protect you from."

"What do you mean someone might hurt us?"

"This area is sitting on a mountain of copper that people who aren't from around here are after. And I'm involved in an investigation that could implicate some very powerful people in this murder."

Jack moved his hands from the fence to his pockets as Aiden flipped his hair out of his eyes.

"You're joking. Someone is coming after us?" said Aiden.

"I hope not, but they could."

"Someone could shoot up the school any day, too, while I'm sitting in class," said Aiden.

"That's a morbid thought, although true. But if you knew there was a shooter, wouldn't you want to go somewhere safe?"

"I think I'd want to stay and protect my friends."

Jack thought this was an honorable comment. It was a remark he wasn't sure he would have heard from Aiden a few years ago. It made Jack stand taller.

"Who would be dumb enough to go after the Clearwater police?" Aiden asked.

"I don't know who they are, and I don't think they're from Clearwater or even know if they're from the states. And I get the impression that the police or even the FBI don't matter to them. We have to be smarter than them, and they're ten steps ahead of us right now."

"Why don't you arrest them?"

"I wish we could, but justice is slow. So until we know for sure what's happening, it's been recommended that we go into a precautionary lockdown."

"Just us or everyone?"

"Right now, just us."

Aiden looked back at his coach and teammates, who were still occupied.

"I met some of these people this afternoon. If I didn't think they were a real threat, I wouldn't be here," said Jack.

"I'm not running from people. I'm not staying locked in your house."

"We wouldn't be at my house. I'm staying at the Ramada Inn with a team of others until I know we're safe."

"What others?"

"An FBI agent, Doris Lewis, Trenton, me."

Aiden checked the location of his coach again, who was still busy helping the freshmen with their backhands. And as long as girls were talking with his partner, no one would miss him.

"Those people sound boring. Have you told Mom?"

"No. And I'm not even going to try. I'm letting you decide."

"Why do you think these people killed the guy in the park?"

"I don't have time to explain it all, but it seems it's because they're willing to kill for what they can't legally get. It seems like that's what they do."

Jack dipped his head and kicked at a piece of gravel on the pavement.

"I've been skeptical of all of this too, so I get that you want to sort it out for yourself. You're old enough that given this information, I have to trust you'll make the right choice. The one thing I've learned over the years is not to push you."

Jack walked toward his truck.

"I have to talk to Mom first," said Aiden.

"No, you don't. She uses you as a weapon to get to me, and

that's not fair to either of us."

He turned around to face Aiden but kept walking backward toward the truck. "Does Mom still have the pistol she took from me?"

"Yes."

Then Jack questioned for a moment if he should continue with the conversation. But Aiden was almost eighteen, and Jack had taught him how to shoot when he was eleven or twelve.

"Do you remember the lessons I taught you about handling a gun?" he asked.

"Of course."

"Tell me what you remember about handling a loaded weapon."

"I know about respecting what a gun can do. And I know how to shoot. I'm as good or better than you."

"If you decide to stay with Mom, you probably should take it out of the case and oil it up, but don't ever use it unless it's for self-defense. And I don't mean self-defense like taking a gun to a protest looking for a fight," said Jack, turning away. "And it sucks that I have to tell you this because there are too many other constructive things you should focus on than having to defend yourself against something I can't begin to explain. You know where to find me if you need me. Please be on the lookout, and be careful. I love you."

CHAPTER
Ten

ON THEIR OWN

The lobby of the Ramada Inn was quiet. Miranda sipped a raspberry margarita and stared out a tinted glass window into a courtyard filled with exotic plants and a koi pond. It was approaching dusk. A few travelers moved luggage in and out. Most people were passing through to other destinations, but a few who saw camping as a miserable experience stayed a couple of nights at the hotel to spend time hiking or fishing and kayaking at the surrounding streams and lake at the state park. And the way people spoke and carried on with laughter as they discussed dinner plans and the next day's activities, none of them seemed to have heard about any lurking danger. Maybe they had just arrived in the area and didn't know a man had been killed the day before, or perhaps they were choosing to ignore the violence because they'd become accustomed to it making the daily national and local news. Miranda never wanted to be one of those people who didn't care. She also missed those brief days of experiencing what it felt like to believe some magical force other than herself was present to do the dirty work to ensure she was safe.

When she heard the automatic door slide open, she immediately sat up, placed her drink on a round glass table, and turned to look at the entryway. When she saw Jack and Trenton, she jumped up, folded her arms, and gently rocked her body back and forth as she waited. A slight smile spread across her lips.

"After we separated at the park, I wondered if it was a good idea. I was starting to think I should come looking for you," she said.

Jack felt her eyes pulling at him even more than before. "I stopped by the station to talk with Steve," Jack said. "You've been right about everything."

"I wish I had other talents than always being right about how the minds of criminals work," said Miranda.

As Jack introduced Trenton to Miranda, Trenton thought it was an unusual and intimate way for a county detective and an FBI agent to greet each other. He'd noticed Jack staring at her for a moment. Miranda was pretty and naturally drew attention to herself through her beauty, but the attention was unsolicited, and Trenton thought it was impolite to stare. But for all he knew, maybe they'd known each other and worked on another case before. Or, more likely, they'd experienced something traumatic that day.

Miranda took a moment to study Trenton. He was thin, gaunt even, suggesting his diet consisted of grains and salads, and he was dressed in khaki pants and a yellow checkered shirt. Miranda didn't like stereotyping people, but Trenton was exactly like she imagined he would be. He fit the description of many environmentalists she'd come across.

"I wish we were meeting under better circumstances, Trenton. How much did Jack tell you?" she asked.

"As much as he could," said Trenton. "But I get the feeling he couldn't tell me everything and was withholding something."

Jack scanned the lobby.

"Where's Doris?" he asked.

"She's in her room," said Miranda. "Being temporarily

evicted from her home was a lot for her to process. Where's your son?"

"Finishing up tennis practice. I tried talking him into coming, but he refused. He's being a teenager who's gone through his parents' messy divorce."

"Hearing from you that he could become involved in a hostage situation didn't convince him to come with you?" she asked.

"You have to consider this is a kid who's grown up with lockdown drills and school shooters. And it wouldn't have mattered what I told him. I did everything I could."

Having spent the day with Jack, Miranda was bothered that his son didn't respect him enough to listen to him. But she realized maybe she'd misjudged Jack as well.

She chose to say nothing more about her concern for him and his son and instead turned her attention toward Trenton. She couldn't control every aspect of people's lives, although, in this case, she wanted to. But she was happy to see that the number of people uniting, aligning themselves with what she saw as the forces of good, was increasing.

"The bureau hasn't cut off my credit card yet," she told Trenton. She extended her hand and offered him a keycard to a hotel room.

"I've been targeted before but never thought I'd be framed for murder. And I never thought I'd become a refugee in my hometown," said Trenton.

She placed the keycard in Trenton's hand and clasped his fingers tightly around it.

"I'm sorry for all the attacks and accusations they've already made against you," she said. "But for them to attack you is proof that you must be a threat, so it's kind of an honor in a way."

As he gazed at Miranda, Trenton could feel the warmth of his blood pulsing through his veins. He took the keycard from her and put it in his pocket. He was beginning to understand why she caught Jack's eye.

"I wish we could all sit at the bar and celebrate that everyone's safe, but the day isn't finished yet," said Miranda.

She led them to a relatively vacant area with more lounge

chairs and a couch. She didn't feel like being driven into hiding in their rooms; there was more privacy where she led them.

"Jack, how did your department handle you telling them the truth about Trenton?" Miranda asked.

"Not well. The only reason Steve released him is that he's hoping Trenton turns out to be the killer so he can come out on top."

"I wish I were surprised," said Miranda. "But it's going just like we thought it would, and I don't have any better news."

Miranda said this without sounding apologetic. She slowly fell back into a chair. Jack and Trenton each took a seat on the black leather chairs as well. The lobby remained empty for the moment.

"There's no other way to say it than to put it out there. I called my supervisor, and we're being denied the resources we need," Miranda confessed. "We're not getting wiretaps, and they're unable or unwilling to help photo ID the guy, even though the FBI has a database of 640 million people."

Jack waited for the punchline, but it never came.

"You're kidding," he said.

"I explained Ethan Richards at the mining company is most likely behind it all, and that's when he got funny. Apparently, they don't want to help us connect this guy in the photo to Ethan Richards."

Jack stared at her. Even though she'd prepared him for this moment, he was speechless as he replayed everything she'd just said.

Trenton had moved to the edge of his chair.

"What did you mean by photo ID-ing someone?" Trenton interrupted. "What photo?"

"We have a photo of a guy who we think is shouldering your gun to and from the murder scene," said Miranda. "All we need to do is find him, and you'd be free to do as you please. But until we find the killer, they still might try to blame you."

Trenton checked for a reaction from Jack before turning back toward Miranda.

"Jack, show it to him," said Miranda. "He's involved in this as much as we are, and unless we have video of Ethan Richards shooting David Willis, no one in my department will care where this is going. There's too much money involved, and they won't risk their careers."

"Explain why your department isn't going to assist us," said Jack. He was infuriated at her confession. The uncertainty of assistance had been a concern he'd been carrying the entire time they'd been together that until now she'd casually dismissed.

"I told you getting support might be questionable when dealing with this company. Show Trenton the photo."

The worried look on Miranda's face was convincing enough for Jack to let go of his rage and do whatever she'd asked. He knew he couldn't be mad at her for holding onto hope because he'd done the same. He leaned back to pull his phone from his pocket. He found the picture they'd retrieved from Doris's trail camera and gave the phone to Trenton.

"I know you find this shocking," said Miranda, "but politically appointed nominations like those made in the FBI make a difference, and you're seeing the effect of it right now."

Trenton used his thumb and forefinger to expand the picture on the screen so he could focus on the weapon better.

"It looks like my gun, minus the silencer," he said. "And that means that asshole was in my house. But what am I supposed to do if we're not getting help from your department and if Jack's department is convinced I'm the killer?"

"That's why we need to have this talk," said Miranda.

She turned to Jack.

"How much did you tell him?" she asked.

"I didn't have to tell him much. The only thing I didn't tell him was that we had the photo. He figured out the rest."

"We didn't want to issue a warrant until we got clearance," Miranda explained to Trenton. "We were hoping we could use wiretaps and phone records to catch Ethan Richards discussing David Willis's death and a plot to take the state park, but that's no longer an option. And now they won't even assist us with figuring out who the guy in the photo is, so we're definitely onto something."

Trenton handed Jack his phone, leaned back in his seat, and folded his hands in his lap while Miranda waited to hear his thoughts.

"So they're cutting you off from assistance because they're afraid of what you might find," said Trenton. "And they feel better off staying out of corporate battles for land."

Miranda's face remained unchanged. Her indifference suggested to Jack that she agreed with Trenton. She almost seemed relieved they were having this conversation.

"You're saying they don't care about prosecuting corporate crime," said Jack. "That seems like something you should have told me earlier."

"I told you how difficult this was going to be. The influence of big business on the department is a trend, and we have to find a way around it," Miranda said to Jack. "It doesn't mean I'm abandoning anyone. I haven't gotten on a plane and left, even though I wanted to. They killed someone to cover something up, so we still have the law on our side. We just have to find another way to get to them."

Trenton leaned forward as he took off his glasses. He repositioned himself in his seat, but no matter what he did, he couldn't get comfortable. He'd lived in the area for most of his adult life, although not nearly as long as Doris, and he'd seen such apathy in government while working for the state inspecting and removing leaking in-ground fuel tanks that had contaminated groundwater. Some people he worked with back then were willing to overlook infractions if they were paid under the table. But the apathy Miranda was talking about was on a scale that could impact an entire region, although it didn't surprise him.

"We need to see for ourselves if there are orchids," said Trenton. "It's the only thing left that we have to connect anyone at the mining company, other than the guy in the photo, to murder."

"But even if we find orchids and can link it to the guy in the photo and to a motive designed by the mining company, we still aren't going to coax anyone to investigate a billion-dollar company," said Miranda.

"Do you want to give up?" asked Jack.

Miranda cast Jack an exacerbated look.

"That's what I'm asking you because my department's stance now impacts us all. The goons sent to Doris's were sent there for a reason, so they're still trying to keep something hidden. And they're gambling that their bullying tactics will be enough to stop anyone from opposing them. And so far, in the past, it's probably worked for them. Their power is now impacting the bureau's decision to back off this."

Jack felt his throat tighten.

"We've just been stripped of our power," he said. "We have no way to arrest Ethan Richards."

"We can still arrest him. We still have our badges. If we find orchids, then we have the chance to shape public opinion in our favor. I don't see this as being over."

Trenton and Jack stared at her, surprised by her casual indifference but Miranda never blinked.

"I'm suggesting we stop seeking approval from people who have no business being in law enforcement," said Miranda. "But all we have is the four of us, and now that word is most likely getting out that we may be onto them, it's difficult to know what opposition we might find by going in and looking. The goons at Doris's said they were asking people like Doris what they knew about the area. They're worried about someone finding something, and I'm guessing it's all about orchids. Environmental protection laws are still in place. So it might help David Willis's cause if we prove that orchids are still there and publicize it."

Jack and Trenton absorbed the seriousness of what Miranda was saying and appeared apprehensive about what she was asking. Trenton was the first to agree to the request. But then Jack remembered Doris telling him he'd been brave by doing something unpopular such as breaking away from his grandfather's expectations. He suspected his decision to continue the investigation with Miranda without the full support from the FBI wouldn't sit well with his department, but after talking with Steve that afternoon, he really didn't care.

Trenton rose quickly, as though he'd suddenly remembered that he needed to be somewhere else, even though their meeting wasn't finished.

"You do understand the danger in this?" said Miranda. "Based on what we've seen from Jack's department, I'm not expecting any help from there either, not that I want it because they'll only muddy things up."

Trenton turned around and lifted his head to speak to her. He saw the warmth in her eyes again.

"Jack thinks highly of you, and I trust you. And if you're part of why I'm not sitting in a jail cell, I'm in. It's been a long day, so we should get some rest."

"We might be exposed to extreme scrutiny depending on what we find tomorrow," Miranda cautioned. "Anything that happens is going to fall on us."

"I'm already being scrutinized and abused for speaking out in favor of saving the environment and for trying to live a quiet life, so nothing you can say scares me. I'll see you both in the morning."

There was quiet after Trenton got into the elevator. In light of everything that had happened, Miranda and Jack felt content for the moment knowing the other was there. When an elderly couple came through the sliding glass door on their way to the parking lot, the unassuming couple held hands, even though they were well into their seventies.

Miranda had seen too much in her life and knew she could never live a life filled with joyful bliss. She felt those days were long gone.

"You knew all along you didn't have the support of your department," said Jack. "Why didn't you make that clearer sooner?"

"I tried to tell you when I said we were in a war, but you weren't ready to hear it. It's only going to get worse moving forward if we happen to find orchids. And what if you had to kill those people today? Is that something you're prepared to do? Because moving forward, there's a real chance we might have to."

Jack removed his cap and pushed his tousled hair back before putting it back on.

"If these people killed David Willis to keep something hidden," said Jack, "then I'll do whatever they force me to do to uncover it. They can't travel the globe thinking they can come into places like Clearwater and kill people to get around following laws, frame people like Trenton, or drive people like Doris off her land. I'm not going to let the justice system fail these people."

"You and I didn't fail anyone."

"No, not you and me."

Miranda studied Jack's face like she'd done this morning. Even in what felt like defeat, he looked handsome.

"I'm glad you've decided what kind of detective you were meant to be," said Miranda.

She handed him a room key.

"We should keep up appearances that we're still attempting to go at them using our department resources. If we're not getting approval for wiretaps on my end, see what happens on your end. Maybe run it by your supervisor, and get your Bill Winslow guy to ID the suspect in the photo through your department. I'm lying low in my department. I'll try to continue to make the appearance that we're all working together and doing what I was told. That's the game we have to play to make it look like we're still team players."

Jack replayed everything he'd seen and done the last day and a half. It was a short thirty hours from first rolling over David Willis's body and seeing the lettering carved into him to where Miranda had now led him.

Miranda got up and moved to the elevator.

"If we find orchids, then we continue wherever that takes us. But if we don't find anything, we find and arrest the guy in the photo and wrap this up. And I'm afraid getting into that park tomorrow will be a test of our commitment. I hope no one tests us, but if it happens, we have to be ready and okay with whatever follows."

"I'm with you," Jack said.

Miranda caught herself gazing at him longer than she intended.

"Thank you for saving my life today. And thank you for rescuing Trenton. You shouldn't have had to do either."

CHAPTER
Eleven

SEARCHING FOR ORCHIDS

Jack sat on the bed in his hotel room. He could hear every sound the people were making in every room around him—the shower water running, the sliding of coat hangers, the scraping of silverware on dishes. He'd known all morning something wasn't right with the way Miranda had been behaving with her talk of Aruba, and now that she'd confessed they wouldn't have the help he expected, he understood the weight they were carrying.

He drank from his glass of whiskey from the hotel bar, then swished the ice cubes around. It was his third drink, enough for the room to feel like it was moving and sufficient to relieve the stress from the day. He remembered wanting to discuss David Willis's drinking with Miranda early in the day. Now he scoffed at the idea.

It still didn't register to him how anyone could deny Miranda help until he thought about the people like Steve in his own department who seemed to have something personal against logic and listening to someone of lower rank than him. But regardless of receiving assistance or not, the choice to move forward and search the park had been made. He felt it was the right choice, and he had been a part of making it, and he was proud of that. But thinking back to the confrontation at Doris's, anything that might happen to them while exposed in the woods he would now own as well. It wouldn't only be on Miranda.

He trusted Miranda but wished she'd been even clearer about them having to solve this case themselves. He continued to question the lack of support. And then he had a crazy thought. Why did it matter if they had support or not? When it came down to it, no one would be so foolish to challenge the authority of the FBI, not in today's civilized world. Attacks on the FBI and the police only happened in movies or other parts of the world.

He even began to question if the guys he'd fired upon at Doris's would have done something as serious as shoot back at them. After a long day and a half in the field, he assured himself his mind was failing him for him to consider anyone would try harming them. Lying on the bed in his hotel room, he listened to the sounds coming through the walls. It reminded him of how astute his hearing was in the early morning woods of every gun deer season when he knew he was among other hunters who didn't always check their line of sight before shooting.

He'd finished a light dinner, and now the plate, silverware, and napkin sat on the end of the bed. He put the glass on the nightstand and concentrated on the text to Steve.

If people like you don't wake up and stop believing lies and accusing people like Trenton, this town and this community, including the lake and the state park, will be nonexistent. I'm attaching a photo of the killer, so you can help identify him, but it doesn't end with this guy, so don't show it to anyone. You can thank me when you see me. Trenton Fuller is off the hook.

Jack pressed the blue send arrow. He reached for his glass of whiskey again and took another sip. He checked to see if he'd missed any messages from his son, but there was nothing. He put down the phone and was about to close his laptop, but he stopped himself. He'd always hoped for a better relationship with his son than he'd had with his father and grandfather. His grandfather was gone, and his father was at odds with him over his career choice. And there was also no reclaiming the days he'd lost arguing with Aiden's mother about countless mundane things.

He typed Aruba beaches into the search bar. There again were the calming images Miranda had been looking at. He was starting to feel the warm water pulling at him, even though he'd never been there. Even though it had only been a day and he barely knew her, and even though she was younger than him by ten years, his eyes lit up whenever he thought of Miranda. He was beginning to grasp why she wanted to run away.

When the knock on the door came, Jack woke up with a jolt, then he felt around in the dark for his phone but couldn't find it. He couldn't remember where the light switch for the lamp on the nightstand was. He didn't think to put pants on when his bare feet hit the carpeted floor. He stumbled through the dark to the door and opened it, and saw Miranda standing in the hallway looking as beautiful as she had the day before. He wanted to reach out and touch her to see if she was real, but he was awake enough to know he shouldn't, though barely.

"Some of us needed a few more hours of beauty sleep," said Miranda. "But it's morning. It's time to get moving."

"I thought about you and what you've been saying about Aruba," said Jack.

"I dreamed of happy things all night, too, like you greeting me at the door in your underwear," she said with a grin. "We're having an important team meeting in the lobby in ten minutes, so jump in the shower and wake up."

Jack rubbed his face and looked at his bare legs as she shut the door.

He remembered the vision of Miranda as he showered and dressed. When he picked up his phone, he saw a text from Steve.

It read, *Call me when you get this, asshole. The guy in the photo is Aaron Pierce.*

Finally, maybe his department was on board. His thoughts

shifted away from Miranda and back to the case. He had to take the time to call Steve.

When Jack finally appeared in the lobby, Doris, Trenton, and Miranda were all pacing near the sliding doors, waiting for him.

"I'm sorry I took so long," said Jack. "I've been talking with my supervisor. They ID'd the guy in the photo, and I filled Steve in on everything that happened at Doris's."

"That's great! You told him everything?" Miranda asked.

"Everything except for the part about me shooting. I didn't think he'd understand that part. And you think he'd be happy that we have a photo of the killer, but he seemed more agitated than anything."

"Because you proved him wrong for wanting to blame Trenton. But knowing the killer's identity is a big step in unraveling the lies," said Miranda.

"Steve agreed to issue a warrant for the guy's arrest. He's got everyone searching for him."

"Maybe it's a sign things in the Clearwater Police Department have turned," said Miranda. "Is the shooter local?"

"No. He's from Florida."

Miranda clutched her phone, wanting to call her agency and have them help with the manhunt. Maybe her supervisor, Blake, had changed his attitude toward her and the case overnight like Jack's supervisor had. Maybe the news that they'd identified the killer would somehow make Blake want to congratulate her and cause him to appreciate all her work, risking her life twenty-four hours a day.

But she relaxed her grip on her phone. She knew Blake was caught in his own battle to remain on the FBI director's good side, which seemed more important to him than she or a town in the Midwest. She had to let go of the idea that help from her department was coming. And if Jack's department was showing signs of helping, it was a sign of the direction she needed to go. Let a local agency show up her branch of the FBI so that any negligence would someday be questioned. She decided that her course of action was now separate from her supervisor's. While Jack's department went after the killer, she and Jack would take the case in an entirely new direction.

Miranda straightened her posture, pulled up a photo on her phone, and held up a colorful picture.

"I have some news of my own," she said.

Miranda handed her phone to Doris so she, Trenton, and Jack could see the image.

"It's an orchid," said Jack.

"It's from Amanda, David Willis's fiancé. It was in Google Cloud," said Miranda. "And it was taken from the day he was killed."

Trenton and Jack exchanged glances.

"You have a photo of an orchid from David Willis's phone," said Jack.

"From one thirty in the afternoon," Miranda clarified. "He must have sent it out right before he was killed."

"Then we know that's why they killed him," said Trenton.

Jack echoed the same conclusion. He looked at everyone's surprised faces. Then he stated, "It's the link to establishing probable cause!"

"I left a message with the EPA," said Miranda. "And it's an orchid that's definitely on the endangered list that mining operations can't disturb."

"Now we can go after Ethan Richards," Jack said. He could feel the tension throughout his entire body ease. He could see an end and feel his bed calling to him. Miranda, more than the others, could understand his optimism. But she wasn't celebrating.

"It should motivate The Nature Conservancy and the EPA to release a statement about the discovery of rare orchids, which should raise suspicion about why a biologist was killed in a state park," said Jack. "And that could give us the political pressure we need to be placed on the DA to investigate the mining company's involvement in the murder."

Miranda's eyes shone, and she brushed back her bangs.

"And who will be pushing for probable cause, Jack? Who's going to dare to try connecting the killer to Ethan Richards? You forget what I told you last night about my supervisor," said Miranda.

Although she wanted to agree with Jack that what they'd uncovered should be substantial, in light of her department's denial to further assist with the case, she doubted the news would inspire the enthusiasm necessary to investigate Ethan Richards. She could see word of one orchid being dismissed as insubstantial when measured against the promises of progress that people like Diane at *The Chronicle* were talking about.

"We're the ones who are going to have to stand up for Clearwater. This entire area is at risk of being stolen from the people who live here. And we don't have time to wait for the EPA," Miranda continued. "Their department has had cuts and changes made to it too, so they're just as vulnerable and overwhelmed as we are. If anything is going to get done, it's going to be on us to do it. If there's one orchid, we should secure the area and try finding more."

Doris gave Miranda a nod of assent.

"Chances are, because of what happened at Doris's yesterday, we'll run into someone today, but I wouldn't ask anyone to do this if I didn't think it was necessary," said Miranda. "But we can stop right now and hope we have enough evidence."

Jack's initial silence suggested he was hesitant, but it only took one look from Miranda to agree with her that they stick to the plan.

"Miranda's right," said Jack. "We need to fully commit to exposing what this company is trying to do in secret, even if we're the only ones willing to do it. We can't rely anymore on other people to put the effort in that we're hoping for."

Doris, who insisted on going with them despite her age and the rough terrain, nodded in agreement. In anticipation of Jack and Trenton agreeing to follow the plan, Miranda had already talked to Doris. Miranda thought because of her age, Doris should have time to process the dangers, so she could have time to decide whether or not she wanted to help. Miranda had cautioned her about the lack of help from her department and about entering the woods and searching for orchids with them that morning. But at Doris's age, she and Miranda felt there wasn't much for her to risk.

If Doris lost the house and the land to the mining company, which they concluded would surely happen by doing nothing or by trusting outside sources with the evidence of only one orchid, Doris's life would already be lost. She'd lose the land that was her life. Doris also foresaw that she'd probably die alone within a year in a nursing home somewhere. The Willis family also would never receive any closure or justice.

"I want to find enough orchids that no one can look away from what these people have done," said Miranda. But then she doubted that enough orchids would ever exist to make people care about this mining company's tactics.

"Doris insists on coming along," she said. "And I've already tried arguing with her, so don't even bother. She knows a little road on the west side, three-quarters of a mile from where the body was found, where she thinks we're more apt to find orchids. Jack, since your supervisor is in such a pleasant mood, tell him about the orchid and that we have a motive for murder. See if we can get some bodies to help do a bigger search and seal off the area. It's worth one last try."

Jack moved away from the group and called Steve.

Then Miranda asked Doris and Trenton, "Do either of you have a concealed carry permit?"

"More than anything, I got mine to make a statement," said Doris.

Trenton confessed he'd gotten one for a similar reason, to make a point that concealed carry laws weren't only for people who wanted to carry guns openly into supermarkets in order to intimidate others.

"I'll give you each a weapon when we get there. If it comes to it and we meet up with those men at Doris's, keep calm and only shoot in self-defense," said Miranda.

"I've been involved in dangerous land grabs like these before," said Doris.

"What do you mean?" Miranda asked.

"When I was in my twenties, I was a triage nurse. This reminds me of a time when we were evacuating a hospital because our camp outside of Lang Vei was overrun. After that day, I carried a pistol for years."

Miranda's and Trenton's eyes met as Doris shared her experience as a nurse overseas in Vietnam. They both questioned if Doris was experiencing a moment of senility, but her age was right, and based on the professional and sensible way Doris always conducted herself, they had no reason not to believe she was telling the truth. The statement gave Miranda and Trenton a new curiosity about what else she had done in her life.

When Jack came over, Miranda could already read the bad news written on his face.

"Steve said he'd check for wiretap clearance through the county DA, but I felt he was just paying me lip service, and I got the usual run-around when it came to assistance."

"People can die of old age waiting around for others to decide if they represent the law. There are better uses of your time than waiting around for your department to get on board," said Doris. "We should get going before it gets hot."

"I called the park last night and told them to close it this morning and to confine campers already there to the lake and their campsites," said Miranda. "So there should be no one left in the area."

It was decided Doris would ride with Miranda. Jack and Trenton would follow them.

"While you're driving, watch for anything suspicious, like roadblocks or cars parked along the way with the driver wanting assistance," said Miranda. "If I see anything like that, I don't trust it, and I'm going to keep driving."

Jack and Trenton looked at one another and nodded.

There was light traffic on the roads, which seemed unusual to Miranda for an early Friday morning. To Jack, it might have been uncommon if he'd been paying attention. But he was still tired and processing the lack of support and the immense responsibilities suddenly being placed on him. He didn't need anyone telling him what they were doing was right, but the affirmation from authority figures like Steve would have made him more confident. He was beginning to accept he was never going to get his approval.

Two miles from Doris's farmhouse, Doris had Miranda pull over on the shoulder of the narrow one-lane road. Jack checked his rearview mirror, and Trenton checked over his shoulder, then the sides of the road. No one else was in sight.

Miranda got out of her car and came back to speak with the men.

"Doris says this is the place and that we should move to the northeast until we reach a valley," said Miranda. "It feels too quiet out here."

"You said you called the park, so that explains why there's no traffic," said Jack.

"Maybe. But be alert because I don't want to walk into an ambush. No one is dying while securing this area. Jack, you take a rifle, get ahead of us, and take point. I hope everyone's phones are charged. The time to have gone searching would have been two days ago or yesterday morning when the park was full of law enforcement before anyone could have been alerted to what we were looking for. But we missed that window."

They all gathered at Miranda's car.

It troubled Jack and Miranda to see Trenton and Doris arming themselves.

"I hope I'm doing the right thing by bringing them along," said Miranda.

She and Jack quietly loaded their weapons and filled their pockets with ammunition.

"After what's been done to them, there's no way they're going to let us go on this expedition without them," said Jack. "And I'm not going to deprive them of their willingness to assist."

Doris couldn't help but think that years ago, they would have had more people on their side volunteering to scour the park, especially if someone had been murdered. But to have asked for help from the public today, she worried, would have risked alerting others who would have sided with the destruction of orchids. It probably would have led to a violent confrontation before they even started.

"We'll travel as a group, with Jack taking point," said Miranda.

"When civilians have to fill in and do the work of the police," said Trenton, "then we really are living in a third-world country."

After they softly closed the trunk and car doors, Miranda whispered to Jack, "I know you'd feel better with more support, but we're following the law. No one has the right to challenge our being here."

"I trust you, Miranda. This is unusual, and it'd be great if we had support, but it is Steve we're talking about. And your boss sounds like an idiot, too, for leaving you hanging. Someday, when this is over, you'll have to explain the ignorance and apathy to me. And I feel partially responsible for your being stuck here, so be careful, and don't let anything happen to you."

Jack was stealthy like a hunter, leading the others through the woods. He walked with caution, careful not to disturb branches or leaves. The others saw he was good at moving through the ferns and rough terrain, almost as though he'd had some experience in the jungle or some military training.

Miranda, Trenton, and Doris, who slid through the forest equally well, kept watch behind and around them, making sure they weren't being followed.

No one said a word. Even the wildlife was silent. All four of them thought it was unusual.

By eight o'clock, they'd traveled half a mile through the thick ferns and jagged, slippery rocks. Miranda kept a watchful eye on Doris, but the veteran nurse managed herself well in the forest, even at her mature age. Miranda smiled at the old woman's spunk and mysterious nature.

There were moments among them when they each questioned the sanity of what they were doing—sneaking through the outer limits of a state park like they were in a war in the jungles of South America. But there was no denying that the irrational violence and accusations each had seen and experienced in the last twenty-four hours had been real. As they made their way deeper and deeper into the forest, they saw no one, which was comforting. They remained vigilant and reminded themselves not to mistake a rogue hiker or rock climber (or another police officer if Jack's department ever showed up) for someone who might be there to harm them.

Doris constantly scanned the forest for clusters of cedar trees, land contours, rock formations—anything that would refresh her memory as to where they were.

"How much farther do you think it is?" Miranda whispered.

Doris pointed at a jagged rock outcrop as the landscape transitioned from stands of poplar trees to cedars.

"Another eighth of a mile," she said. "The forest floor and canopy are like I remember it."

The spark that had left Doris's eyes yesterday after being pushed from her home had returned. The thought of seeing orchids kept inching her forward.

Jack let the group get within forty yards of him before continuing again. He'd cover for them with Doris's rifle as they came near, and they would return the favor whenever he moved ahead.

After wiping the sweat from his forehead in the cool but humid morning, and as he was about to take a step forward, moving farther into the thick forest, he thought he saw movement on a rock outcrop to his right. He stopped and crouched. He pulled the gun scope to his eye and wished he hadn't seen what he did.

Seeing Jack halt, Miranda, Trenton, and Doris stopped, listened for voices, and watched for movement. Miranda told Trenton to stay with Doris while she crept ahead.

When Miranda reached Jack, she knew full well from how he clutched the rifle and his huddled and defensive posture why he had stopped.

Miranda peeked between the fern fronds and around cedar trees but couldn't see anyone.

"How many are there?" she asked.

"All I saw was one. He's stationary like he's on watch."

"Is he armed?"

"He's holding an assault rifle."

Miranda stretched her neck again to look as far as she could in the direction Jack had indicated without giving herself away, but she could see nothing. They both tucked themselves among the safety of the ferns.

"What do you want to do?" whispered Miranda. "Do you

want to call for backup?"

"I've already accepted that no one is coming to help," said Jack.

"Send a text to Steve anyway," said Miranda. "It's time we started calling people like him out on their negligence and documenting it. We need to keep a record."

Jack texted Steve to tell him they ran into a man armed on the west side of the park, a mile in from Fern Road, and to send more people to help diffuse the situation. He was high enough up on the hill that he had decent enough service to send the message.

After the message was sent, they waited for several minutes, but Jack didn't receive a response.

"We could de-escalate this right here if Steve would let me know if he's sending more people," said Jack.

"I'm beyond my limit of giving people like him chances," said Miranda. "If the department and that guy up there prevent us from completing our investigation, they're obstructionists. And if this guy is here on watch, they could be in the valley destroying evidence if there are orchids here. I've never understood why it's so difficult for some to follow the rules."

Jack stared into her blue-green eyes and hoped there was a different solution. Even though Jack had fired upon the men at Doris's, he hadn't intended to kill. He felt fortunate that the men had been smart enough to step aside and leave the women alone. But this confrontation with a gunman standing on a hill guarding or defending something on public property had a more serious feel to it.

"This is unfortunate, but when I got here, I told myself I wouldn't back down if our departments bailed on us. If I back down now, I might as well turn in my badge because what good is it if we can't stand up to criminals," said Miranda.

"I don't know why Steve's not sending assistance," Jack whispered. He looked at his phone again, but there was no response from his supervisor.

Then Miranda did something Jack didn't expect—she kissed him, and he hadn't had time to react.

After Miranda let go, she said, "This is the job you and I are being paid to do, and I know you're from this area, but sometimes police detectives beyond Clearwater have to use deadly force. It's time someone stood up to these people because they've grown so accustomed to a lack of confrontation that now they think their behavior is acceptable. I'd be willing to bet Ethan Richards intentionally sent these people out here to mess with us, so be ready."

There was too much going on in Jack's mind to analyze everything happening. The way Miranda remained calm and composed made him feel she was much older than him.

"I'll let him know I'm with the FBI, and we'll see how he reacts," said Miranda. "If he really is armed, it's time to see how willing they are to use their guns. I'll try talking him down, but if he shoots at us, do your job as a detective of Clearwater. Send these people a message that our government is still functioning and that they're in opposition to it. And send a message to Ethan Richards and the people who should be here with us that no one's going to steal the state park as long as we're here."

Miranda signaled to Trenton and Doris to stay put. Then she looked at Jack one more time before racing off through the saplings and underbrush toward the hill where Jack had seen the man.

Jack immediately reached for her to pull her back toward him, but he was too late, and what good would it have done? She was right about needing to confront this man and maybe kill him if need be. He checked the phone again to see if Steve had responded, but still, there was no answer. Time was again moving too quickly. Maybe he should have spent more time yesterday at the chateau taking Miranda's discussion about Aruba more seriously. They could have been on the beach together sipping pina coladas by now.

He whispered Miranda's name, but she wouldn't have looked back even if she'd heard him.

He watched Miranda slink through the ferns toward the hill, being careful not to alert anyone of her presence.

Jack frantically pulled the gun scope to his eye. This time he could see the guy on the hill had the rifle slung over his shoulder. So far, he hadn't been alerted to their presence. He was turned in the other direction, probably watching over the valley where they'd been headed. *And why did he have a gun, and why so early in the morning,* Jack wondered. *To take by force a state park, something that wasn't his? The guy had to be delusional. He wouldn't dare test them,* Jack thought. But he knew, as Miranda did, that any man who would carry a gun into a state park was already testing the boundaries of the law. And he and Miranda had come to the park to do their job of re-establishing authority while looking for orchids.

The pace of Jack's heartbeat quickened. He felt sweat droplets forming on his forehead. The hope that this would be an easy excursion to gather up orchids and that afterward, everyone could go home and celebrate over drinks and then get some rest was disappearing.

Jack searched for a steadier position. He found a semi-comfortable spot between two saplings concealed in the ferns where he could steady the rifle, giving him a clear shot if necessary. "This makes no sense. Do you really have a death wish?" he whispered. He wanted to shout at the man to put his weapon down, but that would most likely lead to a shootout, which he was still hoping to avoid. His best hope was that maybe Miranda could talk some sense into the stranger.

When Miranda had snuck within forty yards of the man, she carefully and quietly drew her gun from its fabric holster. She struggled to find her badge, but when she did find it in her pants pocket, she moved toward a cedar tree and concealed herself partially behind it.

She thought about all the times she'd pulled her badge on someone. She'd done it so many times now that it was routine. And what had been the purpose of calling out "FBI" other than to make an arrest legal or to give the perpetrator a chance to do the right thing, which rarely happened. But she knew that following the rules of law and stating the truth set her apart from people like the man before her. It's also what separated her from Ethan Richards and from people who failed to stand with her.

"FBI! Lower your weapon!" Miranda shouted. She stood

slightly out from behind the towering cedar, but only enough to where the man could see her.

The man immediately spun around to see who'd shouted. He was wearing army fatigues that had patches of the American flag on them. It took him a moment to find Miranda. He was higher up on the ridge than she was, so he was looking down at her, which gave him the advantage. When he saw Miranda had a gun, which wasn't pointed at him but instead hung benignly from her hand, pointed at the ground, he ducked behind a boulder.

Miranda hoped it was one of the same men she'd met at Doris's yesterday or the man in the photo, but it wasn't. The more men she didn't recognize, the deeper the organization went.

"What are you doing in a state park with a weapon?"

But the man didn't answer. He took his rifle from his shoulder and clicked off the safety. He didn't drop it but clung to it like someone would a lover, which Miranda found disheartening. Then the man found the dangerous end and pointed it in her direction, which she accurately predicted would be his next action. There was no question now about what he was doing there.

Miranda had already moved safely behind the tree by the time he had fully raised the scope of the rifle.

"I said FBI, and right now, you're threatening a federal officer. I'm here with friends to secure the park, so put the gun down," said Miranda.

But the man kept his gun aimed in her direction.

"I have orders not to let anyone past this point," said the man.

"You're on public property. You can't be up there threatening people," said Miranda.

"Ethan Richards and my AR-15 say otherwise."

"I know the name Ethan Richards. He sounds like an ass to me and not someone worth listening to if he convinced you to stand out here with a gun to represent him. Is he around? I'd like to talk to him. And don't you find it odd that he's probably not here sticking his neck out with you?"

"Why are you here?" the man asked.

"It doesn't matter why I'm here. You can't stand up there and hold a gun on people."

"I'm only threatening people who threaten me and my beliefs," said the man.

"I don't understand how I'm the one doing the threatening. What are your beliefs?"

"Progress is under attack, and I'm here to defend it."

"So standing up there threatening me is defending progress, and everyone who disagrees with you is wrong?"

"Yes."

"That's an archaic and barbaric way to think, and it isn't protecting progress. And it's going to get you into trouble when you run into someone who isn't afraid of you or your threats. Drop your weapon so we can talk."

"We are talking, and I listen to Ethan Richards because he stands for progress."

There's that awful name again, Miranda thought to herself.

"Progress isn't standing on a hill, taking something that isn't yours," she said. "Drop your weapon and come down here so we can talk. You're trying to prevent us from searching the park, but taking that position is not only stupid, it's illegal. And I don't want to see anyone get hurt. Least of all someone who's caught up in something they don't understand."

The man didn't respond right away, and the delay gave Miranda hope. She felt, as she did with most people, that she and the man would have a lot to talk about if they could just sit down together and have a few drinks at a bar.

"What's your name?" Miranda asked, trying to re-establish a connection.

But the man suspected she was using a police tactic. Had he lowered his gun, maybe he would have taken the time to understand she was sincere.

"I can't let you search the valley," said the man. "We were told to stand out here and send a message to anyone looking for orchids who doesn't support the mining company."

"Who told you that? Ethan Richards?"

"I can't say."

"You're just blindly following whoever told you to intimidate and be a bully. I don't know what kind of insanity that is, but you'd better snap out of it."

Miranda thought there might be others just like him in the woods who were hearing them talk and who, in time, would surround them.

"Surrender your weapon and come down here so we can talk at the police station about who sent you here. Those are the people we're after, not victims of the propaganda like you."

Miranda moved farther behind the tree and checked her peripheral. Her breathing intensified.

She could see out of the corner of her eye that Jack was rock steady, already locked onto the man like he was nothing more to him than a paper target.

"Last chance to drop the gun and turn yourself in peacefully," said Miranda.

"I'm staying where I am and doing the right thing for my country. I'm not going to let a cunt like you interfere!"

The insult fanned the blaze already burning within Miranda. To ignite rage was always the intent of spewing the word, and Miranda was aware that it was nothing but an attempt to get her to do something irrational. But instead of firing her weapon and rushing at him, which she wanted to do, she calmly said, "I don't know if you understand what you're doing or saying. Ethan Richards isn't the friend you think he is. He's not the type of person who's going to be there when you need him. Put the gun down, and let's talk."

There was silence for a moment, causing Miranda to think her passive response had gotten through to him. Then, without any further warning, the man pulled the trigger repeatedly on the AR-15 semi-automatic rifle, firing at the tree Miranda was standing behind.

"Police!" Jack shouted.

The man fired two more rounds in Miranda's direction before spinning around to fire at Jack. When he did, Jack squeezed the trigger.

The moment Jack saw through the scope that the man had fallen, he shouldered his rifle. "You stupid prick!" he yelled.

Then he raced toward Miranda, nearly stumbling at the thought of what he might find.

When he got to her, she was sitting on the ground behind the tree. Jack could see no blood on her, no sign of a wound or injury.

He knelt beside her, grabbed her arm, and looked her over more thoroughly. He couldn't find anything physically wrong with her.

"Is he dead?" said Miranda.

"I think so. It was a clean shot."

Miranda threw her arms around him. "I'm sorry you had to kill, but there was no getting through to him."

"Why did he shoot?"

"Because he'd been drinking the Kool-Aid that Ethan Richards had been giving him, and he thought he owned the place. He'd been misinformed that the law didn't matter, and it's too bad he didn't listen, but if this has to happen to bring attention to what's going on here, then so be it."

Trenton and Doris began creeping up the hill toward them. Miranda signaled with her hands for them to hold up. As she did, she and Jack could hear men talking above them and to their left, farther to the north toward Doris's far-off farmhouse.

"We can't risk letting them see Doris and Trenton," Miranda whispered. "We need to get around them, flank them, and lead them away. Kill every one of them if you have to in order to protect the others. We are officers reclaiming recreational state property, Jack. Don't let anyone make you think otherwise."

She kissed him on the cheek.

Then she was off again.

Jack scrambled to get above the men they'd heard. When he reached the height where the body of the man he killed lay, he nudged the man with his foot as he stepped over him. He'd recognized the face when he'd had the scope on him but was too confused and angry to feel remorse for the man as he lay lifeless from the fatal wound to his head. He had seen the man firing at Miranda as if she were an insignificant character in a video game, and as he discovered, such complete disregard for her life was enough to get him to do something he never thought he would. It made no sense to Jack that the man had opened fire on them only to defend his apparent belief that the park was his to take.

Before he reached the peak of the hill, he heard Miranda shout, "FBI!"

She'd barely finished shouting when Jack heard gunfire bursts again. He instinctively flinched, but he heard no bullets zing past him. The thunderous sound of the gunshots was close. But then he realized from experience that he would have heard the bullet whistling through the air or felt it ripping through his flesh before the sound of the gun report if they were shooting at him. The gunshots were coming from his left, just over the hill.

Jack frantically moved to where he could look down on the shooters. He saw Miranda sprinting, ducking, weaving her way through the ferns. In a millisecond, Jack's brain reminded him that this was Wisconsin and not the jungles of some foreign country.

Jack swiftly moved into position behind the two men shooting from the hip, not even aiming with any precision, in Miranda's direction.

"Police!" he shouted. "You need to listen!"

Neither man showed signs of listening as they spun around and took aim at him. But Jack immediately put a bullet through each man's chest.

As the gunfire moved farther away, Trenton and Doris huddled out of sight among the ferns.

"I should get up there and help," said Trenton.

"We have to help in a different way," said Doris. "We might not get back to this area again. And now that I'm getting my bearing, I think it's this way."

She didn't bother concealing herself now as she moved toward a rock outcrop she remembered from when she was young. After returning from war, where she served as a triage nurse, she sought solitude on long hikes into the valley, carrying her paints and canvas, but it had been years since she'd been to this exact location.

"We have to stay low so they don't shoot us," Trenton whispered.

But Doris stood tall like a seasoned veteran assessing which way to go on the battlefield on which her side had already declared victory.

"The orchids are this way," she said.

Trenton could hear the woods grow quiet as he looked up the hill where Jack and Miranda had gone. When he checked back in Doris's direction, she continued moving swiftly along the path toward the rock outcrop. He did his best to keep up.

The valley floor was carpeted with ferns among a stand of towering cedars. It was like walking five hundred years ago through an ancient forest. The air smelled crisp and untainted by pollutants. Above them on the cliffs, there was still no sound from Jack or Miranda.

"We should be up there helping," said Trenton.

"Focus on what's in front of you," said Doris. "The flowers are purple, egg-shaped, and they're a fragile, shy-looking plant, so we'll need to go slow so we don't overlook them. We should spread out to cover more area."

There was no deer trail to follow now. Trenton drifted left as Doris directed him. But when he saw how quickly the old woman began moving to her right almost instinctively over rocks and pools of stagnant water, under half-fallen logs, and through the ferns like she was twenty-something, he knew he needed to stay with her.

"She's from another generation," he said in awe.

When he caught up with her, Doris had stopped in a small shaded glen underneath the cedars amid the jagged rock formations.

Trenton didn't have to ask her why she had stopped. When he saw it, a look of bewilderment spread across his face.

"It would have been nice if our governor hadn't eliminated broadband from the budget," said Doris. "One of us should be in the background for scale. And we should use both phones so we don't lose the photos."

Hundreds of fragile white and purple flowers were in front of them, mixed among the green ferns and red jack-in-the-pulpit seeds. The forest floor looked like a life-size Monet watercolor painting.

"You've known about this place all your life?" Trenton said in a whisper. He couldn't look away from the sight as he felt all of his pockets for his phone.

"Those can't be real," he said.

Doris handed him her phone so he could video her walking among the orchids.

"I've known of people finding some occasionally in remote pockets on the other side of the park, but I've always kept this place quiet, and it's been easy because it's so remote. My guess is the mining company heard the rumors too, and they were worried David Willis stumbled upon something he wouldn't keep to himself. I shouldn't have kept it quiet all these years either."

"Why didn't they destroy it all?"

"I suppose that's what the guns, the lies, and the killing were for. They had to make sure no one would look for the orchids and find them. It was all meant to discourage people from looking for them in the first place so they'd disappear from people's minds forever," said Doris.

Then she stooped down and brushed one of the many purple flowers with the back of her hand. It felt like silk, just like she remembered.

"Start shooting video," she said. "And then let's see about getting out of here."

CHAPTER
Twelve
THE OPEN PRAIRIE

Jack was already blaming himself for shouting at the men before shooting them. The two or three seconds it had taken him to yell meant that another three or four rounds had been fired at Miranda before he silenced their guns.

As he rushed to find her, he blamed himself for not believing her when she suggested the area was at war. He had ignored all the signs, such as her lack of license plates and how she never wore any FBI markings, which now indicated to him she didn't want to be singled out and targeted as a law enforcement officer. It signified a general disregard for the law among the public, which he'd just witnessed, as well as how far her status had been eroded within her own department. He'd been dumb. And now he'd lost sight of her after focusing on killing the shooters after she'd tried talking them down. He called out to Miranda but received no response. He hoped and trusted the silence was because she didn't want to give away her position. He couldn't bear to think of the other alternative.

Jack leaped and bounded among the forest of cedars while clutching the rifle.

When he got to Miranda, she was sitting upright against a tree with her trembling legs stretched out in front of her. She was clenching her teeth in pain, inspecting the rip in her pants on her right thigh where blood was seeping through.

When Jack saw the blood, he instinctively slung Doris's rifle over his shoulder and knelt beside her. Without asking, he grabbed her pants near the wound and was about to rip them open so he could see the injury better.

Miranda grabbed him by the wrists to calm him.

"These are my favorite pants," she said. "It's nothing."

But judging by the amount of blood on her pant leg, Jack wasn't convinced.

"It's not nothing. We should look at the wound before you determine how bad it is."

"It hurts more when there's shrapnel left inside or if bones are shattered, and this doesn't feel like that. And it's probably not a good idea that we're both here together," Miranda whispered.

Even in his panic, Jack could process from her description of the wound that this wasn't the first time she'd been shot.

"We'll take care of me later," said Miranda. "We take care of Trenton and Doris first, then us. It's what we do."

Jack could see from the calm in her eyes she was attempting to make him feel everything was alright. Or maybe it was her training as a field agent reminding her to put others before herself. He still wasn't convinced she was okay, but it was clear when Miranda pushed him away she wasn't going to let him look at the wound.

"We can't keep moving if you're hurt," Jack whispered.

"I told you it's nothing. And right now, we need to know how many more there are. We need to keep moving away from Doris and Trenton."

Miranda knew if she could keep Jack focused on the task of getting them safely out of there and not on her, his sense of logic would return.

"Are there any behind us? Did you miss any?" she asked.

"I didn't miss any. Can you walk?"

Jack reached to assist her, but he could see the defiance in her building, suggesting that he'd better retract his hand or lose it.

"I'm not going to let you carry me out so you can feel my ass," Miranda said playfully, trying to bring humor to the tense situation. "Stay focused."

Jack felt his phone vibrate. Even though he fumbled to take it from his pocket, he was surprised that his hands weren't shaking more than they were. When he looked at the phone, his eyes widened.

"They found orchids!" he whispered, tilting his head in disbelief as he studied the text message. "During the shooting, they must have snuck off alone. They're not saying how many, but they said to meet them back toward the vehicles."

"Doris must have found them," Miranda said. Then she scanned the forest ahead of them. Jack reflected on the men he'd killed.

"We can't stay here," said Miranda.

Jack knelt in the dirt and slipped the sling of the rifle over his shoulder.

"Somehow, they predicted we were going to be here. And if they called in more patrols to the park," said Miranda, "they probably would have found our cars by now. Waiting at our point of entry for us to return is something they'd do. And I can see that creep we met yesterday being sneaky like that. Did you check the bodies?"

"They're locals," said Jack.

They hadn't killed any of the men from yesterday, but Jack knew the names of the men he'd just killed. They were often in trouble with the law. And they were vocal supporters of the mine only because they were told to be.

Jack considered that none of the articles he'd ever read stated the number of jobs the mining operation would bring, whether the community members would get the mining jobs, or how much money the jobs would pay. But these men jumped on board with the claims that the mining operation was the community's savior and were willing to kill people and an endangered species to silence everyone else's voice.

Jack felt so enraged at the men for being so gullible that their names didn't even matter.

"I don't trust this," said Miranda, her eyes scanning the now silent woods. "They could have more waiting for us back at the vehicles. I think we abandon the cars, keep moving in the direction we're going, and get to Doris's farmhouse. I think it's our best chance."

Jack texted Doris and Trenton to head in their direction.

"Give me one second, and then I'll lead the way," he said to Miranda.

When he finished texting, Jack looked at her leg again, but he knew not to ask if she was okay or not to help her stand up. Remembering what she'd said earlier, if she wanted help, she'd say so. He touched her on the shoulder as a sign of reassurance that everything would be okay or as a final goodbye in case they ran into more crazy radicals. He disappeared ahead of her into the woods and moved quickly among the cedars, rocks, and ferns.

The moment Jack was gone, Miranda winced and tore open her pant leg. She forced herself to look at the wound to make sure she wasn't fooling herself about how bad it was. She was relieved to see a half-moon crater a little more than the diameter of a bullet gouged out of the skin on her thigh. As she had determined before, the amount of blood exaggerated the extent of the wound, but it burned like a wound opened to the drying wind and sun. She was grateful Jack had silenced the men before they'd gotten more rounds off.

When she got up, the muscles in her leg constricted, but she tried not to wince this time. She stood among the rocks and plants and could see Trenton and Doris working their way toward her. She couldn't see anyone pursuing them. The direction Jack had gone was silent. She texted Jack, who immediately responded by texting back, *All clear.*

The bleeding from Miranda's leg was beginning to stop, and color was returning to her face. Jack's response that the woods were clear ahead made her feel her instinct to avoid returning to the vehicles was right, although she didn't want to become overly confident.

But the more she thought about it, the more she could see someone like Ethan Richards or the goons she'd met at Doris's stirring up misguided locals to start a skirmish, which would push them back to their vehicles where the real guns would be waiting in ambush. She always questioned if she was being paranoid, but maybe her paranoia was valid and was what kept her alive.

Doris and Trenton didn't stop to inspect the bodies as they hurried past them. And when they got to Miranda, all three regrouped and moved swiftly in Jack's direction.

Whenever Miranda surveyed Doris to see how she was handling the terrain, the more Doris reminded her, at least to some extent, of her aunt back in California. Having Doris with them, an undaunting peer with a strong moral compass, reminded Miranda how much she had missed her aunt Rita and that maybe she'd been too harsh toward her for trying to steer her away from becoming an FBI agent.

When they reached a clearing at the end of the state park boundary, they all breathed a sigh of relief at the sight, suggesting they might actually make it out of the woods alive. Where the edge of the woods finally met the tall field grass, Miranda and Jack could see across the prairie where they had run the UTV the day before in search of cameras. And far off in the distance, they could see Doris's three-story Woodland home. To their right sat an old, rusty Chevy truck parked at the state park boundary fifty yards from them. There was no one near it.

"We're going to get you out of here, Doris," said Jack.

Doris smiled between breaths and said, "I got to see the orchids one last time, so not much matters anymore."

The fatigue of a well-lived life and a quick-paced two-mile excursion showed through the lines on her face.

"A couple of us should go ahead and get a vehicle," said Miranda.

Jack's eyes were drawn to the bloodstain on Miranda's leg, and she could feel him looking, but she didn't acknowledge his concern.

The others hadn't noticed her leg yet. They were busy guessing the distance to the farmhouse. There was a quick discussion about if anyone would be there waiting for them. They all agreed that the truck to their right was probably from the men Jack had shot and killed. But they also didn't dismiss the possibility that there were more of them. And whoever had driven the truck had to have driven across Doris's property to park it where it was.

Jack ran over to the truck to see if the keys were in it, but they weren't.

When he told everyone, Doris said, "The car in the barn works."

"Where the hell is Steve?" said Jack. "Someone certainly heard all of the shooting and reported it."

"Hand me your phone, Doris. We need to send the photos to get word circulating so everyone knows why we were here."

Trenton was already texting with both thumbs, sending photos to people in his contacts.

Doris handed her phone to Miranda, who used it to send the photos to herself. She sent the photos to her boss and the EPA when they were finally uploaded. A national newspaper contact was among the other contacts in her phone to which she sent the photos.

"There's no question now as to why David Willis was murdered," said Jack. "What more evidence do people need?"

"A confession of their involvement, which will never happen," said Miranda. "But we made our point that we know exactly what they're trying to keep hidden and that some of us in law enforcement won't be intimidated."

Trenton finally noticed the blood stain on Miranda's leg.

"You're hurt."

"I swear you and Jack have never seen blood before," said Miranda.

Doris didn't want to exacerbate the concern by rushing over to her. She trusted if Miranda were seriously injured that she'd say so.

"I'll run to the house," said Trenton. "Miranda can't, and Jack, you're the best with a rifle."

Jack surveyed the open field ahead of them.

"That's a thousand yards across from here to the house," Jack said. "I can't protect you from that far. We should move together as a group."

"Remember, Doris is with us," Miranda whispered to Jack. Then she told Doris, "Doris, help Jack look after me."

Miranda ran into the clearing before anyone could stop her.

Knowing he would never catch her even though she was wounded, Jack scoped the land ahead of her. Doris took the rifle from Trenton and did the same as Jack.

Running across an open prairie where there might be shooters was like being dragged by a riptide into the ocean, Miranda decided. The wind on her face made her remember when she was ten, lying across the surfboard, feeling as though she would be easy prey for the sharks as she drifted beyond the break into deeper water. The more she paddled and panicked; the farther out the sea dragged her. Only by remaining calm and paddling gradually south with the current did she break free from the tide's grip and from being lost in the ocean.

She gritted her teeth now as she found her rhythm and raced across the prairie. Her breathing calmed. After she left the cover of the forest to get to the distant farmhouse, she could feel Jack's presence as he scoped the landscape to protect her. The pain in her leg began to subside.

When Miranda reached Doris's yard, she canvassed the area to make sure no one was nearby. The keys to the UTV were still in it, right where she, Jack, and Doris had left them the day before. Miranda was catching her breath and just about to start the UTV when a Clearwater police SUV came slowly down the driveway. The strobe lights were turned off. The ground was already dry from yesterday's early morning rain, so hints of dust were churning in the air behind the vehicle as it approached.

Miranda felt the throbbing pain in her leg again, reminding her she didn't want to get senselessly gunned down. Still out of breath, she climbed out of the UTV, took out her badge, and held her hands in the air.

The police SUV stopped some distance away, and two men jumped out and drew their pistols.

"FBI," Miranda said. "We could use your help."

She stood steady with her hands held up.

The officers began walking near her with their guns still drawn, and for a moment, Miranda questioned their intentions.

But when they got close enough to see the badge, the officers lowered and holstered their weapons.

"We received a report of gunshots in this area," the deputy on the left said. He was short and twitchy. He could see the blood on her jeans.

"There's an armed militia in this area trying to steal property for a mining operation," said Miranda, lowering her hands.

She explained that she and Jack had killed three men firing on them. And then she said she had to get the others she'd left behind in the woods. She told the deputies to get their rifles out of the vehicle in case a gunfight erupted from the tree lines. Then she asked them to wait near the house and cover her.

Back in the woods, Jack, Doris, and Trenton scanned the tree line as Miranda raced the UTV across the field toward them.

Doris turned to Jack and said, "The absence of leadership in law enforcement has given some people in this area the impression that they're the law, so you did the right thing. You saved the community today from being stolen by warmongers."

But how the community and even the rest of the country would react to the news that three locals had been killed by a law enforcement officer within a state park sat uneasily with Jack.

Trenton didn't care how the community viewed it. Although he was angry at such stupid men like those Jack had killed, who apparently stood guard in a state park and shot at officers because they were brainwashed to do it, he was happy to finally be involved in some payback.

When Miranda drove up to them, Jack was the last to get in. He placed his hands over her wrists and removed her hands from the steering wheel and looked her in the eye.

"Don't ever do that again without talking to me first," said Jack. "You could have been killed. I couldn't cover you that far away."

"I appreciate the concern, but arguing over who would do it

wasn't getting us anywhere, and it all worked out," said Miranda.

As they were busy bickering, Trenton helped buckle Doris in.

Miranda already had the UTV in reverse before Jack closed the door. And within seconds, the four of them were racing back toward Doris's across the grassy plateau. It was anything but a joyride. Even though Miranda covered the terrain at record speed, the time it took to travel across the exposed ground felt like an eternity. The uncertainty of what came next weighed heavily on all of their minds.

When they arrived at the farmhouse, Miranda and Trenton helped Doris out of the front seat, walked with her into the house, and led her to the couch while Jack headed toward the deputies.

"We need to put something on that wound," said Doris, looking at Miranda's leg as she was helped to the couch.

But Miranda placed her hand on Doris's shoulder. She was focused on getting Doris to rest.

"You're worried, aren't you, that we're not out of this yet," said Doris.

Miranda didn't have to say anything more for Doris or Trenton to understand that nothing in terms of their safety was finalized, even with proof of more orchids.

Jack ignored their questions as he approached and pushed his way between the two deputies outside. He continued his hurried pace over to their police cruiser. He opened the door and grabbed the radio handset.

"This is Detective Jack Calaway," he said. "Send the coroner and the Use-of-Force Review Team to Doris Lewis's. Three men are dead."

CHAPTER
Thirteen
CONSEQUENCES

Jack swung open the door and stormed into Steve's office. He stopped in front of the desk, and Steve, who was sitting, looking over baseball stats in between preparing a statement for the media about the deaths in the park, reached behind himself for his baseball bat. He then spun his chair around again so he was facing Jack. He held the handle of the bat in one hand while resting the barrel in the elbow notch of his other arm.

"What the hell are you doing?" said Jack.

"Thinking about what I'm going to say to the media."

"Do you even understand what your refusal to have any law-based stance on what's been happening around here has done?" shouted Jack. "Sitting behind your goddamn desk and not sending any support is the same as granting them permission to take whatever they want. And now they think killing us is okay if we challenge them. I repeatedly asked for help this morning, and where were you?" said Jack.

"I was talking to the DA and the attorney general about how

we should be handling this case."

"All you would have had to do was show a display of unity. If you'd have shown up with the entire police force, those men might have backed down, and they'd still be alive."

"Do you understand the situation you put me in?" Steve finally reacted. "Do you know who you killed today?"

"Three idiots who got caught up in something they shouldn't have," said Jack.

"It was the Petersen boy and the Jameson brothers," Steve clarified.

"I know who they are, and why is it that because they're local, you're willing to excuse what they've done? They made a conscious choice to shoot at a federal officer and to take the side of a criminal who works for the mining company, but you're choosing to defend them instead of me. That says everything anyone needs to know about you," said Jack. "And I can bet because you and the DA are too much alike, we're not getting wiretaps or phone clearance on Ethan Richards, even though we now know exactly why this mining company had David Willis murdered. There's an entire field of endangered orchids here that they're trying to keep off everyone's radar so they can steal the land!"

"You're not getting phone taps because the DA agrees this is one we should sit out. And I'll need your gun while this goddamn mess is being investigated!"

"I don't have to give you my gun until the review team says I did something wrong, which I didn't. And my feeling is I'm gonna come out okay in this because we had killers in the state park shooting at a county and federal officer," said Jack. "And if anyone is in trouble, it's you for sitting here on your ass, allowing it to happen!"

"You better watch it, Jack. I'm not alone in thinking you crossed the line."

"That's not the impression I'm getting from the people concerned with solving this case. And apparently, the Petersen boy threatened one of the review team's family members earlier this week, who happened to question the mining company's intent. That's all they did was question this mining company's practices, and he went off on him. I was worried about what the investigators might say, but they treated me like the responsible detective I am, almost like they appreciated that I did my job and didn't suck up to this mining company."

Steve came at him from around the desk like he was going to attack, but Jack snatched the bat like he was taking a toy away from a child.

Steve went back behind his desk.

"Fuck you, Jack Calaway! I outrank you!"

"Then act like it and use your position to do something! Otherwise, you're in a leadership role you should have never been given," said Jack. "It's vacant."

Then he stopped talking. Continuing this conversation was a waste of breath, he decided.

He laid the baseball bat on a chair and stormed from the room, leaving the door open.

As he walked through the building toward the exit, he calmed himself as everyone in the office stared at him. Before he exited, he turned to everyone in their cubbies and said, "Jayden Peterson and the Jamesons died today because they were defending the people who we suspect killed David Willis, and they were trying to keep the FBI and me from discovering endangered orchids so the mining company can steal the park."

Jack ran his fingers through his hair.

"In case any of you care, it appears that the mining company looking at the site to the north is secretly trying to take this entire area, including the lake, to get at the copper. If these people who were killed today who stood beside Ethan Richards are the people we choose to defend and not the people like David Willis, Doris Lewis, or Trenton Fuller who stand for truth and transparency, then I don't belong here."

As he was leaving, he turned and said, "I'm not sure if Steve told anyone, but he has a picture and name of the guy who killed David Willis. So do your jobs and help find him. And send out an APB and plaster that photo everywhere, including in the supermarket entrances and on telephone poles. And if you find him, call me, and make it clear that no one shoots him because we need to talk to him to find out Ethan Richards' involvement in this."

Jack waited for someone to say something, but no one did. He decided to let them consider on their own what he'd said.

On the sidewalk outside, he texted his son:

You might have already heard, but if not, I'll probably be in the news, so be prepared for it. I want you to know I've done nothing wrong in spite of what your mom will probably tell you. Love you. Stay safe.

Then he jumped in his truck.

Before leaving the station, he laid his head on his arms as he clung to the steering wheel.

CHAPTER
Fourteen
HEALING

In her hotel room, Miranda had finished washing the remnants of dry blood from her leg. Sitting on the bed and looking at her injured body, she refused to cry. She would now have another scar on her body, and she knew she was lucky yet again to have escaped a potentially fatal situation. She felt indifference to the senseless loss of life because she'd come to accept that killing was necessary when people were so entrenched in a distorted reality. She didn't regret having pushed the issue. She'd driven herself to the hospital to get stitches. She'd left Jack to deal with the review team and dropped Doris off at the hotel.

Miranda smiled and unfastened the lock when she heard Jack's voice as he knocked on the door. Then she remembered that she was wearing only underwear and a T-shirt, and the pain from the wound on her leg caused her entire body to tense. She had a white bandage on her thigh where the bullet had carved out the chunk of skin. She thought about covering up, but even though she and Jack had only known each other for a few days, she felt more comfortable with him than with guys she'd dated for months. She sat on the edge of the bed and crossed her legs, but she could feel the skin pull tight where the bullet wound had been stitched, so she uncrossed them. She didn't want the sutures to tear.

Jack hadn't seen a woman wearing so little in a while. His mind was already full, trying to make sense of all that had happened that day. He didn't know what to make of Miranda sitting on the bed. He wondered if he should go to his room, but he wanted to be close to her because she'd risked everything to help his community while his department stood by and did nothing.

But under the circumstances, he questioned how he could be close to her without making it sexual. Or maybe that's what Miranda wanted. She'd been touching him the last two days. And she'd kissed him before she'd run off into the woods. But Jack had made relationship blunders in the past.

He didn't want to assume this beautiful young agent could feel an attraction to him, an older, sometimes mystifying county detective, especially so soon. Maybe the affection she'd shown him the past two days was out of stress and anxiety. Or perhaps she was half-naked because she simply didn't care if he saw her that way after the ordeal they'd been through.

To be safe and to quiet the noise in his head, Jack grabbed a chair next to the bed and moved it against the wall, diagonal from where Miranda sat. It created the right amount of distance, allowing the question of her skimpy attire to go unanswered.

He asked Miranda if she'd gone to the hospital to get stitches, which in hindsight, seemed obvious. She said yes, and he told her he didn't like being separated when he'd had to return to the scene where he'd done the killing.

"How did your talk with the review team go?" he asked.

"It was pretty short. I gave them my interpretation, and they seemed receptive. They knew I needed to get to the hospital. What about you?"

"It went fine, but Steve wanted me to turn in my gun until they clear me of any wrongdoing," he said.

"He had no right to do that," said Miranda.

"I told him I wouldn't hand it over unless the review team made me."

"He's throwing his weight around now because he knows he should have been there."

Miranda could tell by the furrows on Jack's forehead that he was struggling with having had to kill, along with the repercussions of waiting around for judgment. This was routine to her.

"Steve and most of the others are still figuring out which side of this to land on safely," said Miranda.

"They're supposed to support the law."

"But he doesn't. He doesn't have the strength for it, which is part of the problem. I don't know how he ever passed you up, but the community and department need people like you because you're willing to stand up to these people."

Jack quieted after Miranda spoke. She was becoming a solid voice of affirmation and reason among the chaos. The way she was able to justify what they'd done was enough to take his mind off the blame for killing three local people. He looked at Miranda's thigh and then the bandage. He tried not to let the fact that she was sitting in her underwear affect his behavior. But it was obvious by his constant shifting that he was restless and couldn't get comfortable.

"Do you want me to get you something?" said Jack.

"I'm fine. I took some pain medicine. The scar will match the rest of my war wounds. It's another chapter in my unending book of adventures and injuries."

Jack searched her legs and other parts of her body for other scars. None were visible. But he noticed her legs were shapely and toned, just like he imagined.

"When I left the office, I asked to have an all-points bulletin sent out describing the killer because I wasn't sure if Steve had done it. I shouldn't need to remind everyone it wasn't us who started it, but it felt necessary."

"I said this was an unusual case. Hopefully, the EPA is paying attention to my messages and knows they have our support, and it's enough for them to start their investigation."

Miranda crossed her legs again, but she could feel the stitched skin pull taut, so she put her foot back down on the carpeted floor.

"I sent word about the orchids to everyone I could think of outside of my department, mainly to the EPA and reporters," she said.

She saw from Jack's stare and the way he stopped fidgeting there was more on his mind than the case.

"I used to take more time talking people off a cliff," Miranda said. "But they don't listen anyway, and then I endanger my life by giving them a chance to redeem themselves that they never take."

"I know now why you talk about Aruba," said Jack. "The moment you got here, you saw how maddening this case would be. But you stayed anyway. You're better than any of the people I work with. You're probably better than anyone in your department."

They could hear a maid rolling a laundry cart down the hallway through the closed door. Both of them went silent and fixated on the door.

They turned to one another again when the noise disappeared.

"As word gets out, it's a waiting game now to see if anyone will pressure our departments to conduct a more thorough investigation," said Miranda. "But the other thing that could happen is Ethan Richards might try diversion tactics to smear us by using the media to label us as job killers. They'll try to encourage a mob to come after us to make it all go away in an attempt to erase everything they've done. These are the games I tried warning you about. They'll flood social media with propaganda to take the heat off themselves."

"I know you warned me, but nothing you ever said could have prepared me for it."

"Hopefully, when word gets out, the people of Clearwater who understand what happened today will be grateful for what you did. But it is lonely waiting for that approval. And sometimes people don't vocalize it, but it's there. I'm sure David Willis's family will appreciate what you did."

"All I did was pull the trigger. You're the one who got us this far. I should have trusted you from the very beginning."

Jack got up suddenly and walked into the small kitchen area.

"Where are Trenton and Doris? We should all be celebrating exposing the lies and drawing attention to the area," he said.

"Trenton said something about turning over the information to lawmakers who will listen. I doubt it will work, but we have to keep trying because even though today was a victory, it will take more than us to prosecute Ethan Richards."

"Where is Doris?"

"She went to rest and to do some painting now that we could bring some of her art supplies from the house. She said that seeing the orchids again took her back to the days of her old boyfriends."

Miranda and Jack laughed at this thought, and neither doubted it was true.

"I've been holding myself back from saying what I want to say to you," said Jack. "But before I say something I'll regret, I should probably go."

"You can say whatever you want, Jack. I needed to set parameters initially, but I think you understand why."

"I understand too many people have hurt you."

Then they became quiet. Neither of them was interested in hearing any more about Trenton or Doris.

Jack opened the small refrigerator and saw it was empty. As he closed the door, he turned toward Miranda, who sat with her back to him. He could feel his throat tighten.

"This is going to sound dorky, but I don't know that I've ever met anyone as fascinating as you," said Jack.

Miranda looked over her shoulder.

"When we met, I was expecting a remnant from the Cold War," Jack went on. "Someone older who didn't get moving until eleven in the morning."

Miranda got up from the bed and turned to face him.

"I had expectations of you, too," said Miranda. "But you've come a long way from our discussions yesterday morning. After our talk at the park chateau, I was ready to leave."

Jack felt himself wanting to run his hand through his hair, but he resisted the urge.

Miranda pulled at the fringes of the bandage on her leg. "You don't know how refreshing it is to have someone understand all I've been through and realize I'm not crazy," said Miranda. "I'd have left after we found the photo if you were just another ordinary detective, but you trusted me and stood by me when other people caved under the threats and the pressure."

Jack stayed by the refrigerator as she came near.

He touched the sides of her ribs as she draped her arms over his shoulder and around his neck.

"I'm ten years older than you," said Jack.

"Are you worried about having a heart attack?"

"I'm worried this is moving too fast."

"After what happened today, you're more concerned about differences in age than compatibility? You've passed any test or vetting process I can think of giving you. You stood up for your community and for what's right at the risk of endangering yourself, and there's nothing more seductive than that."

When Miranda lifted her T-shirt over her head, Jack could see the scar on her right shoulder where it looked like a bullet had passed through. It wasn't recent, but maybe three years old, he thought. Four or five inches lower, and it would have pierced her heart. He touched the scar softly with his fingers. He noticed other wounds on her other shoulder and another on one side of her lower neck that her shirt had hidden. He wondered if she'd been strangled at some point.

"Ever since my divorce, I'm not good with relationships," said Jack.

"If you divorced, you probably weren't good with relationships before the divorce. But maybe you've improved since then."

Jack kissed her scars and her lips.

Then he slowly, softly kissed her breasts.

Miranda felt weak in his grasp. She unfastened his pants and pushed him onto the bed.

"Are you sure you're up for this?" said Jack.

"I'm not going to let a little wound prevent me from enjoying myself and being with someone who could make me happy. I won't let this job or these people control every moment of my life."

When Miranda returned from the bathroom in the middle of the night, Jack, who was sound asleep, had rolled toward her side of the bed. His right arm rested on the warm sheets where her body had been, as though he'd been searching for her. He slept soundly and without worry.

Miranda slid into her spot and propped Jack's arm across her bare chest, careful not to wake him. Then she laid on her side and turned her head to face him, so she could watch him breathe. She hadn't taken a risk like this in a long time, but right now, she was glad that she had.

She was smiling, picturing boarding a plane to Aruba with Jack, walking arm in arm, laughing as they do in the movies. She imagined him struggling to put luggage in the overhead plane compartment. Then she saw his phone begin lighting up and buzzing on the nightstand like it was receiving a distress signal.

She considered ignoring it, but it wasn't her message. She put her hand on Jack's shoulder and shook him until he was awake.

"Go back to sleep," he said. "We need our rest."

"It's three in the morning, and someone needs you," she said.

The phone lit up again as Jack picked it up and rested his back against a pillow propped up against the headboard. He rubbed his eyes.

Miranda rolled out of bed and started getting dressed.

The text read: *There's a guy here who says he has Trenton Fuller's gun. He wants to talk.*

When Jack saw it was from his son, Aiden, he jumped out of bed. His fingers couldn't move fast enough as he dialed. Then he waited and waited, but his son didn't answer.

"Who is it?" said Miranda.

Instead of responding, Jack tried calling his ex-wife, but she wasn't answering either.

"Now isn't the time to ignore my calls!" he shouted.

He tried texting with both thumbs the way his son had shown him, but he had to start over. Using his index finger was faster: *Keep him cornered and don't touch the gun.*

CHAPTER
Fifteen
NEW HOPE

Miranda squeezed into a sports bra, slipped into black dress pants, and put on a white compression T-shirt with a zipper. Even though she didn't always wear the FBI markings, she always dressed well. Her aunt Rita had taught her the way one dressed demonstrated a level of self-respect. And even though the same respect wasn't often returned to her, the way she appeared confident even when she wasn't particularly self-assured was sometimes enough to intimidate criminals.

The more Miranda thought about the time spent with Aunt Rita, the more she realized her aunt had done everything she could to make her strong and successful. She realized Rita had loved her the only way a stand-in mother could. Maybe she'd judged her aunt too harshly after leaving to become a detective. She hadn't understood back then that Aunt Rita had only wanted the best life for her.

Miranda looked over at Jack, pulling his shirt over his angular shoulders and toned biceps. She knew now that when she first saw him, she'd judged him quickly and unfairly, but that was part of the self-preservation game that resulted from jumping from case to case, location to location. Looking back to the morning they'd met, she knew she couldn't have treated him any differently than she had.

"I'm not sure what this means," said Miranda.

"This has to be a setup," said Jack. "Maybe Aiden has a gun pointed at him and can't answer the phone. I should have sent him away when you told me to, but my ex-wife would have issued an Amber Alert."

"It wasn't my place to get in the middle of it. I only knew that at some point we'd draw attention to ourselves," said Miranda. "We knew what we were doing was risky, and now we have to get ourselves out of this, which we will."

"You were only trying to look out for me, and I didn't see it," said Jack.

"We don't know what this is yet, so don't panic."

But Miranda wasn't sure Jack had heard her.

When they were both dressed, Jack insisted on driving his truck because he could get to the house faster.

They scanned the parking lot for suspiciously parked cars before hurrying to their own.

Before she got into the truck with Jack, Miranda took some guns from her Camry. She placed them on the truck seat and buckled herself in.

"Before we try and figure out what last night was, we have to go back to the way things were. We have to control our emotions and show no fear—at least while working. In moments like these, we have to be as ruthless as they are, and that's a part I hate. We can't afford to be vulnerable or filled with emotion," said Miranda.

"The killer is with my son, so, of course, I'm vulnerable."

"I mean with us. We have to take a deep breath and not let our minds get the best of us; otherwise, we'll do something stupid, and then they win. The possibility of a killer willing to confess, if that's what this is, isn't something we can ignore. It might bring us one more step closer to indicting Ethan Richards or whoever else is involved. There's no doubt it's a result of what happened yesterday. It's completely unexpected, if that's what this is—someone wanting to confess. But that's what scares me because I've never had anything like this happen to me while working a case. If I seem worried, it's because I'm confused about why the killer would turn himself in now. I'm not as concerned about the safety of your son because, judging from the text message, it sounded like he was in control."

Jack understood there was no going back to the innocence he knew only a few days ago.

"If you're not sure about this, maybe we should try again to get your department involved," said Miranda.

Jack didn't even bother to look at her.

Knowing he was right, Miranda wanted to snap her fingers and undo this lesson for Jack. Part of the learning curve of working homicide cases was preventing access to your personal life and those in it from criminals. She only hoped this lesson wouldn't be too harsh.

"There's no explanation for him to come to us now because the orchids have already been exposed," she said. "Unless they turned on him for some reason."

Jack took his ball cap from the dash and put it on his head.

"I don't know what this is either," said Jack. "Other than it means our names are circulating for him to find my old address."

"He could be surrendering," said Miranda. "And maybe he didn't go to the station because he doesn't know who to trust. I think it's odd he admitted to your son about having Trenton's gun. This feels to me like someone who wants to cut a deal."

"Of all the scenarios running through my head, that's not one that jumps out to me, but I hope you're right."

"After yesterday I was hoping our roles in this case were finished. But this is odd. We don't have the authority to offer him immunity for testimony if he is trying to surrender," said Miranda. "And the people who can make that arrangement, like my boss, probably don't want anyone hearing his testimony because of the people he might implicate, so unless things have changed since yesterday, they won't grant him protection. So I'm not sure how to handle this."

The safety of his son was all Jack could think about, but he could sense Miranda was wrestling with this new direction the case had taken. She seemed concerned more than she had been even yesterday when they'd made the trip to the woods. And the way she talked now made it seem like she wasn't concerned they were walking into an ambush, so he questioned how the killer's surrender could be worse than whatever she was imagining.

It felt like they'd just left the hotel parking lot when Jack announced, "It's coming up on the right."

Miranda cleared any lingering thoughts from her mind of sex, love, sleep, and sandy beaches. She hated having to let go of the hours she hadn't thought at all about the case. She tried focusing on understanding why the killer had gone to Jack's ex-wife's house. *Could publicizing the orchids have really created a massive shake-up in the organization?* she wondered. She sat up and checked her pistol to see if she'd put a round in the chamber.

"We're at a delicate point here. Stay calm, and, remember, don't do anything out of anger," said Miranda. But she could see from the blank stare that Jack's focus was on his son and that he probably hadn't even heard her.

"Do you want me to go to the door instead?" she asked.

"I need to do this for my son," said Jack. "But if something happens to him, no one will have to worry about finding a way to prosecute Ethan Richards. And if we never have anyone on the side of the law supporting us, I'm starting to wonder if we shouldn't take matters into our own hands anyway."

"I worry about the lack of support all the time, Jack. But before we go rogue, take the time to hear this guy out. Everything we've done so far has been right, and it's led to this moment where the killer is contacting us," said Miranda. "It could be bad, but he could also lead us to Ethan Richards. We have to trust the law; otherwise, we're no better than them, and we are better than them. Look at what they've thrown at us, and they haven't been able to stop us yet."

Jack took a deep breath and then slowly let it out. He knew she was right again.

When Jack slowed to a stop far down the street, Miranda got out before they could even see the house.

"It's too early to understand the implications of everything that happened yesterday. It could be a hostage situation, but it could also be a sign that we're getting to them and that people are turning," she said. "Let's do this right so we can get back to the hotel and order in for breakfast. And then we can talk about last night and what your plans moving forward in law enforcement are. He might have chosen to come to you out of respect."

"I don't believe that."

"You should. You're more respected than you give yourself credit for. I noticed it the way Doris first looked at you. I agree it's a stretch, but he might be entrusting his life to you. We'll know in a few minutes."

Miranda closed the door.

She hid in the shadows and followed the truck slowly up the street until she found a spot next to a neighbor's garage where she could scan rooftops and alleyways and watch safely and be unseen.

Jack slowly crept the truck ahead and parked down the street. He dismissed what Miranda had said about respect, but he re-membered everything else she had said—Aaron Pierce probably wanted to confess and implicate others in exchange for immunity. It boosted his confidence because she hadn't been wrong about anything yet. But he wasn't about to take any chances either. He left the vehicle, drew his pistol, then used the shadows to conceal himself until he reached the front door. He stood to the side of the door as he knocked.

To Miranda's surprise, as she watched from the shadows, Jack lowered the gun a second later and stepped aside as the door opened. The man in the trail camera photo stepped outside, es-corted by a young man she assumed was Jack's son, who was also carrying a pistol. Jack grabbed Aaron forcefully by the arm, and he accommodated Jack by turning around and allowing himself to be handcuffed. Then Jack patted him down and took his wallet from his back pocket and his cell phone from his front pocket. It appeared that Jack checked his ID and took the time to read him his rights. Then Jack hugged his son as he ignored his ex-wife, who appeared to be shouting obscenities at him. He escorted Aaron over to the truck and closed the door behind him.

Jack went to his son again, said something to him while handing him a card from his wallet, and hugged him tight. His ex-wife tried separating father and son by pushing them apart, but when she failed to break the bond, she slapped Jack across the face and stormed back inside the house. Jack and his son talked for only a few seconds more.

When Jack finally pulled up to collect her, Miranda opened the front truck door. Her pistol was drawn but dangling from her hand, hanging at her side. Jack let out a heavy sigh when he saw her.

Miranda got in and closed the door.

"Is everything alright?" she said to Jack. "If that's your ex-wife, she has a lot of anger built up toward you."

"She doesn't like me drawing negative attention to the family, as if I have some control over it."

"Is everyone safe?"

"Yes. I couldn't have done this with anyone else," said Jack. "You and I really need a break when this is all over."

"You made the arrest look easy. You and I are learning to do just fine without a SWAT team," said Miranda.

She gave Jack a smile and a nod before turning her attention toward the man in the back seat.

He wore camouflage pants and a tight black T-shirt, two sizes too small for him.

"You fit the same pattern. It's like all of you wished you'd gone off to fight in a war together, but no respectable army would take you, so you brought war here," Miranda said to Aaron. "I don't understand that. And couldn't whatever this is have waited until morning? And what are you doing at a police detective's ex-wife's house at three thirty in the morning?"

Aaron remained silent.

"He said he has information that can help us," Jack interrupted.

"Did you read him his rights?"

"Yes."

Miranda turned again to the man.

"Is your name Aaron Pierce?" Miranda asked.

"Yes. And I know who both of you are too. Almost everyone in this area does."

"What is this about? You're the one we have on camera walking from the crime scene," said Miranda. "You're the one who murdered David Willis, and now you seek out Detective Calaway to terrorize his family?"

Aaron looked straight ahead in defiance, refusing to give Miranda the satisfaction of humbling him.

"Is this a setup?" Miranda asked. "Should we be looking for snipers on rooftops?"

"No," said Aaron.

"Then what is it? Let me see his cellphone, Jack."

Jack gave Miranda Aaron's phone as she'd requested. Then Miranda turned to Aaron.

"Do you have any tracking devices turned on?" she asked.

"No."

"What's your password?"

"Nine, three, seven, one, five, three, nine."

Miranda typed in the code he'd given her, then quickly scrolled through the phone, looking for uploaded or activated tracking apps. She couldn't find any. She set the phone on the seat.

"Why'd you come to Detective Calaway's ex-wife's house?" Miranda asked.

"I was looking for both of you, and if you weren't there, I knew I could get you to come."

"You were hoping we'd show up so you could kill us?"

"I was looking to surrender."

"Why do you want to surrender to us? Why not go to the police station?"

"Because I don't trust anyone there to protect me. I'm not safe because of you two."

"Of course, you're not safe from the law."

"You're both behind the killings in the park," said Aaron.

"Three people were shot for being stupid and firing on officers," Miranda corrected. "That's true."

"Whatever. Word's out that you have a picture of me carrying the gun, and now they're worried I might threaten their operation once I'm caught. And they kill people like me, so it's better for me to make a deal with you now."

"How do you know we're responsible for finding your picture."

"Because it's a big organization with lots of people tracking information on people like you."

"This mining organization is doing that?"

"Yes."

"And now they're threatening you too?"

"Yes."

"So why should that concern us?" said Miranda.

"Because you're law enforcement, and I'm not the only one involved."

"You had an accomplice in the murder?"

"I was told by Ethan Richards to check on David Willis and to remove him if I felt he was a threat to the mining operation."

"Is Ethan Richards after the state park?" Miranda asked.

"Yes. They want this entire area for fifty miles."

"Do you have any proof that he personally told you to kill David Willis, like a recording or names of other witnesses?"

"There are witnesses, but no one besides me will talk."

Miranda paused to process what she was hearing. A killer willing to testify he'd been hired to eliminate David Willis sounded great, but it would never hold up in court without another witness to corroborate the story.

"Without other witnesses, you have nothing," she said. "If you're looking for protection in exchange for testimony, we're not in the business of protecting killers who can't prove the truth to their stories."

"I know more."

"Go on," said Miranda.

Jack looked out the window at his ex-wife's house. Then he rubbed his eyes and held his forehead for a moment before gripping the steering wheel again.

"There's a plan with lawyers and judges and a senator to take the state park and section it off with land to the north," said Aaron. "And I know about it. And the governor and a bunch of elected people are in on it. And I know they're scrambling to keep the killings and the orchids quiet to avoid drawing attention to themselves. And I want protection before I say anything more. You people make deals all the time."

"You're not in a position of power that allows you to barter. There's nothing you can do to redeem yourself for what you've done to David Willis. You destroyed a family."

At this point, porch lights and lights in the nearby houses were turning on. To make sure neighbors knew the police were involved in the disturbance, Jack turned on the blue and red LED strobe lights.

Miranda thought it was too early in the morning to be having this conversation. She willed her brain to focus and look beyond the damage Aaron had caused. If he was telling the truth and high-ranking elected officials were involved, as she had suspected, then why did Aaron think anyone, such as the DA, would ever agree to cut him a deal? Why had he turned himself in? The politicians the company owned would pressure the DA to keep him from testifying. Did he think she and Jack could find a way around the system? Then she remembered that he did misspell forest on David Willis's forehead.

"What deal did they offer you to help their plan to steal the park? How much did they pay you?" Miranda asked.

"It was their promise of creating jobs that brought me up here from Florida. They needed someone at the state to say the area contained no endangered species. David Willis was going to be paid too, but he backed out. He was going to spill the news about the orchids. But looking back, it was all for nothing be-cause yesterday you two exposed the orchid problem."

"So your job was to apply pressure to David Willis to make sure he did what they needed him to do. And when he refused, you killed him and framed Trenton Fuller. And now that the orchids are out in the open, they're going to declare war on you to prevent anyone from testifying that they ever gave you the orders?"

She raised her pistol and pointed it at Aaron's head.

Questioning if she was yet fully awake, Jack leaned toward her to get her to lower her gun.

Just when it seemed Miranda would pull the trigger, she lowered her weapon.

Jack took a breath and let out a sigh of relief. He sat back in his seat again.

Aaron stared at Miranda as though he dared her to shoot him.

"You're one of the most pathetic, saddest people I've ever met," said Miranda. "And I've met a lot of people like you. And because you were dumb, now you're everyone's problem. Drive us somewhere to get something to eat," she told Jack. "I can't believe the number of people brainwashed into doing the dirty work for these people."

Then she changed the conversation because she needed to talk about something more positive.

"How is your son?" she asked Jack.

Jack flipped the strobe light switch off.

"He hugged me. He hasn't done that in years. So he must have been rattled, but he did well considering the circumstances. He said the news was saying I killed three people yesterday, but he wanted to hear my side. I gave him my key card and told him to go to the hotel because the others we met at Doris's are still out there."

"I'm glad he's alright, and I hope he listens and gets to the hotel. Maybe you two turned a corner."

"I hope so. They can come after me but leave my family out of it."

She grabbed his arm and then let go.

"I don't understand how Ethan Richards has such power over these people. I remember when losing the ability to reason was something people tried to avoid."

Miranda went inside the Kwik Trip gas station to get muffins, donuts, fruit, and coffee. The stop would also buy her some time, as she waited for the coffee cups to fill, to think about what to do in light of Aaron's confession. She ran her fingers through her hair and her hand across her tired face as she tried to make sense of everything Aaron had shared.

Outside in the truck, Jack checked every ten or fifteen seconds for the Kwik Trip door to open and for Miranda to return. He'd never had a killer alone in his custody. As he scanned for the slightest movement of the door, he waited for Aaron to berate the police or rant about the unfairness of life. He even wondered if he'd confess about regretting everything bad he'd ever done now that his life was potentially on the line. But Aaron said nothing. He was silent. And in the quiet, Jack didn't want to sit there, allowing Aaron to think he had the upper hand in anything.

"I was one of the first to see David Willis," said Jack. "His parents and fiancé won't get to show him at his funeral because you carved words—words?—one of which was misspelled, into his forehead. Explain that to me because I don't understand it."

"I was never a good speller."

Jack was taken aback for a second by the audacity of the comment. He took several deep breaths to calm himself.

"If that's all you can say about killing and desecrating a person, Miranda is right in thinking that we should get rid of you."

Aaron lifted his head.

"David Willis was too dumb to see that people like him are holding up progress," he said. "And I was being paid to steer any investigation of illegal activity away from anyone at the mining company."

Jack's and Aaron's eyes met in the rearview mirror.

"You're an idiot if you think killing people because they challenge you to think is progress," said Jack. "I keep hearing that word progress. And it's not that people like David Willis can't see that we might need things like mining to stop global warming or that poverty is a problem. They only want a plan moving forward that's best for everyone, not just for the people who will steal and rape the land to profit from it. Making sure everyone is included and discussing what's best for the environment is progress because we only get one shot to get it right."

Jack paused to take a breath before continuing. "You're part of a domestic terrorist group who thinks they're saving the world by breaking laws, but you people are the real oppressors. And now you're turning to us, the law, to save you after the company has bought the politicians who control and dismantle the law for your benefit. So who's the stupid one? I don't care what you have to barter with. There's no saving you, and in a way, I even pity you."

Jack pushed up the rearview mirror so he couldn't see Aaron's face. Then he replayed in his mind what he'd said. He sat up straight as he realized he'd just articulated what had been on his mind the last two days. Then he thought back to what Miranda had said yesterday, that maybe they should end the case right there by turning in Aaron. Now that they had him, maybe she was right.

He thought that if no other departments were helping them, they would have to gain enough public support to go after Ethan Richards and any elected officials working with him by educating a large portion of the population that thought like the people he'd shot in the park, who spelled exactly like Aaron did. That would be a monumental task. But if they ended the case now, and if word about the killings and the discovery of the orchids was silenced by those in the media the mining company owned and enforced, what would become of Doris and Trenton and Aiden? What would become of the orchids and the community of Clearwater? Would anything they'd already done even matter?

But the killer had turned himself in, Jack thought. *The surrender was successful, without confrontation or violence. Maybe it was progress. Maybe they were making a difference by being forceful and violent in opposition to the violence threatening his community. Or perhaps Aaron was playing them.*

Miranda came out of the Kwik Trip doors and jumped in the

front.

"I'm finally starting to wake up and consider what we have here. But keep driving until we figure out what to do with him," she told Jack. She offered him a donut, which he took, then handed him a hot cup of French vanilla coffee.

Then she turned to Aaron. "You told Jack's son you had the murder weapon, so where is it? Let's try starting with that before I decide whether or not to turn you over to your people."

"They have it locked in a safe," said Aaron.

"Who has it locked in a safe?"

"Ethan Richards. I took the key with me before I left, so they couldn't use the gun to frame the guy I took it from. It's in my wallet."

Jack took the wallet from the dash and gave it to Miranda. When Miranda opened it, she saw a gold key among a loose stack of bills.

"Aaron, if you're serious about turning yourself in and making things right, I want you to record everything you told us from the beginning, so it's documented," said Miranda. She pulled out her phone and placed her thumb on the red video recorder button. "We're not the ones who can grant you immunity, so we will have to tell others what you told us. You'll need to convince people you didn't act alone, and because of the money and promises of jobs made by these people, that's going to be a difficult sell. So it's going to be on you to save yourself."

Aaron reluctantly and ashamedly repeated his comments to Miranda while she recorded them. He stated who he was, said that the mining company had paid him to silence David Willis in order to conceal rare orchids and that the gun was stored at a lake house Ethan Richards was renting.

When he was finished speaking, Miranda stopped the recording and typed a message to Blake, her supervisor, explaining that even though the killer had surrendered and confessed, the case wasn't finished. She also said that the truth about everyone who was involved was coming out now, so Blake needed to decide with whom he was aligned—Ethan Richards or the law. Then she sent the message.

"If nothing else, these documented calls and texts for the assistance they keep ignoring will make a good case for negligence and corruption within my department if anyone ever cares enough to pursue it," she said.

Jack noticed vanilla frosting on Miranda's mouth as they turned to face one another. He pointed it out to her. It caused Jack to smile, momentarily removing them from the seriousness of the situation. He also smiled because the new detail about the location of Trenton's gun, if true, along with the surrender of the murderer who was willing to talk, seemed to be the result of the work Miranda and he had done. If the discovery of the orchids wasn't enough to get people involved, which they still questioned it would be, they also now had an informant in their possession who could, at the very least, connect someone at the top of the mining operation directly to the murder. No one could dispute the success of that.

"If we accuse these people of crimes you say they committed that no one else but you is willing to verify, will we be able to find enough information that shows you weren't some radical acting independently?"

"I attended meetings. I was part of their group," said Aaron.

Miranda couldn't hide her frustration as her face turned red. "But that isn't enough, not if you truly want to help us end this. There has to be more than what you're telling us to arrest them as accomplices and convict them. We'll need more than the gun being kept at their place to show their involvement. And we need more than your word that they sent you to kill. We need the one thing they're afraid of. Don't you understand? Jack and I get the impression that no one from either of our departments will care what happens to you. No one will sit you at a table and offer you a plea deal like you're hoping because they're too wrapped up in the propaganda or the deal themselves. And I guarantee that if we put you in front of a camera and you say they pushed you to kill David Willis, a large portion of the public, who also doesn't care about orchids, won't care about you either because the choice to kill was your decision. And they probably agree with your decision to preserve the promise of jobs this company made.

So how do we make them care that your miserable life is worth saving?"

"Take the attention off all of us and put it back on them," said Aaron.

"You saw me message my boss that you have information," said Miranda. "And he's not responding, and he won't unless someone higher up pressures him. You're a victim of the system you helped create."

She held up her phone for effect to show that no one was contacting her.

"You'll have to find the report David Willis drew up," said Aaron. "It's the one thing they're afraid of."

Miranda and Jack tilted their heads at one another to see if the other had heard correctly.

"We already have the orchids," said Jack.

"No, not that. He had a file of everything," said Aaron.

"Who did?"

"David Willis. He documented everything. Dates, meetings, planning, the lawyers, the land tracts they wanted to steal, the senator's involvement, the paperwork, audio recordings, and the newspapers being paid. They were pressuring him to sign off on the park, which is required to get the permits. And he didn't like that his people had put him in that position, so he recorded and documented whatever he could."

"How do you know this?" Miranda asked. "His family never said anything."

"I don't know what he did or didn't tell his family. David warned the company to follow the rules and the EPA guidelines. And the day before I went out to the woods, he got into an argument and played a clip of one of the politicians speaking to Ethan Richards. He was being pressured to do his job and get the permits passed, but he pushed back. And I thought he was going along with it, but then he went off on his own looking for orchids."

To make sure she was hearing things correctly, Miranda asked again if David Willis had physical evidence that detailed everyone involved.

"Yes," said Aaron, nodding to make his point. "If you find the files, we both get what we want."

"You don't get to control this conversation or what happens to you. I know you're hoping the public or a court will acquit you, but I promise you you're going to jail for killing David Willis," said Miranda. "You're lucky Wisconsin doesn't have the death penalty."

Miranda wanted to make it clear to him that moments of remorse didn't excuse or dismiss anything that had already been done. But before Aaron had too much time to think about the consequences of his actions, Miranda knew she'd better press him for more answers.

"Where are these magical files?" she said.

"Ethan Richards thought they were in a safe deposit box," said Aaron.

"Are they?"

"I'm not sure. They've already asked the Willis family if he would have had anything he was hiding at the bank that would have gotten him killed, and no one knew anything. Ethan Richards is clever that way. He gets people thinking he's on their side working with investigators so they give them information."

Miranda and Jack thought back to their conversation with David Willis's mother and how Ethan Richards manipulated and lied to her while she was mourning the loss of her son.

"You haven't learned anything if you think Ethan Richards is clever and not a psychopath for manipulating people's emotions to get what he wants," said Miranda. Then she turned to Jack and said, "We should forget Ethan Richards and concentrate on the gun, so no one can use it to frame Trenton."

"He could be telling the truth," said Jack. "If he is, this is the break we were hoping for. The gun won't matter because he already confessed to using it."

"When something that can expose the level of corruption we're looking at falls into our lap, it's likely too good to be true," said Miranda.

And then she thought, *what if it were really true?* If the evidence was that damning, was it really something they wanted to be involved in exposing? They were already ostracized from their departments. Even though she wanted to talk Jack out of following up on the lead and talk him into dropping Aaron off at the station and finally being free from it all, she couldn't let go of the possibility that David Willis could have been smart enough to have documented everything. She thought of the conversation she and Jack had had with David's mother.

"If you know this information exists, and if it's not in a safe deposit box," said Miranda, turning around again to speak directly to Aaron, "where do you think it is?"

"I don't know where it is. Nobody knows, but I think he left clues on his camera."

"What do you mean?"

"I found numbers on his camera."

"What numbers?"

"Pictures of numbers. He had random photos of numbers in his camera. I wrote some of them down because I thought they'd be addresses. But there are too many numbers."

"You're talking about a puzzle of some sort," said Miranda.

"Yes."

"Do you have his camera so I can see what you're talking about?"

"I took the SD card out of it and threw the camera in the lake."

"What kinds of numerical pictures did you see?"

"He has all kinds of pictures of nature and his girlfriend, and then randomly, he threw in pictures of numbers. They don't fit."

"How can you show me?"

"The SD card is in my wallet in one of the side holders."

Miranda searched his wallet again and came up with the blue SD card. The first thing she wanted to do was make sure it was legitimate and not planted. If she could find pictures of David Willis's fiancé on the SD card, she could have them verified as having come from David's camera.

"You're going to jail," said Miranda. "I want to be clear about that. This feels like a trap because you have much to lose."

"If you don't put the people behind this, like Ethan Richards, in jail, then I lose more than I already have," said Aaron. "So I have as much or more to lose than you do. If you don't have a card reader, I took pictures of his photos using my phone."

Miranda grabbed his phone again, put on her cheaters, and typed in the code he had given her moments ago. She didn't bother to ask him why he hadn't mentioned he'd taken photos using his phone when he'd told her about the SD card, but criminals of Aaron's kind never did think logically. Or was he intentionally messing with her and trying to confuse her? Then she decided it didn't matter because she was interested in what he was telling her, no matter the risk of falling into a trap.

She scrolled through the photos on Aaron's phone until she saw pictures of numbers. The photos could have been Aaron's own, but she could tell they were pictures of other photos from the borders. There was also a time stamp on them. The dates were within days of each other and were from months earlier. There were photos of clock minute hands pointing at numbers, numbers on computer keyboards, numbers of highway markers, pictures of more clock hands pointing at numbers, and numbers of temperatures on thermometers. It all seemed random. And then there was a photo of a garden shed with no numbers mixed among the other photos. There was a pattern, but Miranda couldn't make sense of it.

"What's this garden shed doing in here?" asked Miranda, showing the picture to Aaron. It was embedded among the rest of the photos. It didn't fit the rest of the number collage.

"It was mixed in with the pictures of the numbers, so I thought it might mean something."

Miranda questioned again if he was telling the truth because she'd never met anyone who'd planned a murder who had a fully functioning brain. And the fact that Aaron hadn't spelled forest correctly validated her concerns about trusting him. But then she blocked questioning his intellect from her thoughts as her mind began working. It was almost like someone was telling her the answers to what she was witnessing.

"I know what they are. I saw something like this in a book when I was young. They're coordinates," Miranda said. "The numbers on the thermometers represent degrees, the numbers the minute hands point to are the minutes, and the second hands point to the seconds. Are the photos in order like they were on David Willis's camera?" she asked Aaron.

"Yes."

"But what about all of the other numbers?" said Jack.

"They're fake markers meant to confuse people like Aaron."

"Why not just get a safe deposit box?"

"Safe deposit boxes and safes are the first places people look," said Miranda.

She opened a latitude-longitude app on her phone and plugged the numbers that she'd singled out from the temperature photos and the minute and second hand pictures in the order they were displayed and entered them. She didn't act surprised when the numbers immediately zoomed in on an area not far from Clearwater. She expanded the location on her phone even farther until she could see an address pop up.

"It comes up as a place along the lake," said Miranda.

"Then it's probably planted," said Jack.

"Do you recognize it?" Miranda asked Aaron, showing him the phone through the mesh separating the backseat from the front.

"It's hard to see through the screen," said Aaron.

Miranda pulled the phone away from his sight and held it up for Jack.

"Jack, do you recognize it?" she asked.

At first, Jack was going to tell her no, that at a glance, he didn't recognize the address she'd magically pulled up from the coordinates. He was still amazed by how quickly she'd solved the puzzle. But then, when he actually looked at the phone, he saw the house was just north of Clearwater. He took the phone from her hand so he could zoom out to see the entire town. Then he zoomed the screen back in again. He wanted to make sure there was no confusion about the area he was looking at, so he changed the map to a satellite image.

"I may not be awake yet, but I think that's Jeff's house," said Jack.

"Jeff from *The Chronicle*?"

"Yes."

Miranda turned again to face Aaron.

"Why would information that can potentially destroy everyone in this mining operation by linking them to a murder be at Jeff's house?" she asked.

"I don't know, but I know a guy named Jeff has been accepting money to print stories."

Miranda turned her head away as a sign she'd had enough. Then she took a bite of an apple, took her time chewing and swallowing it, and washed it down with coffee. At Jack's indication that this house belonged to Jeff, she was suspicious of the existence of evidence. But she also wondered if David Willis could have been so smart as to leave behind evidence where no one would think of looking.

Having so much damning evidence tucked away in a garden shed on Jeff's property would be a stretch, but the thought of it was intriguing. It was like mistaking a dead body for a treasure chest on the beach when she was young. Her own mind's deceit was a thought that stayed with her and cautioned her to believe it.

"What was David Willis's connection to Jeff's house?" asked Miranda.

"He'd been sent there by his supervisor to meet with Ethan Richards a couple of times," said Aaron.

"It sounds like there are too many supervisors in positions they shouldn't be in," said Jack.

"We were going to interview Jeff anyway and never got to it," Miranda said, staring directly at Jack. "After yesterday, I doubt we can trust your department to help, so that leaves us to do it all. The time to go is now when no one is awake."

"So what do we do with him? Should we bring him along?"

"In case we would get in a bind, I don't want to be worrying about him. We need to be thinking clearly, and we can't have him talking to people either, so we'll need Trenton and Doris to deliver Aaron to your department as soon as we're in the clear."

"I don't like involving Trenton and Doris," said Jack.

"They've done more than they should have ever had to."

"I agree. But then the other option is to turn Aaron over to your department and let everyone in on it. Let Steve and your district attorney pursue it and risk alerting Ethan Richards. And then you and I have taken this case as far as we can. Or we could bring Aaron along and help him get a lesser sentence for cooperating and assisting us."

When Miranda phrased it that way, Jack wrapped his arms across the top of the steering wheel and rested his head on his hands. Then he leaned back and sat up straight.

"I don't understand why this doesn't concern more people in law enforcement than us. I hope we don't regret this, but if we do nothing, everything else we've done is pointless. And I hope this isn't too assertive, but when this case is over, I'm flying you to whatever beach you want to visit, and I'm coming with you."

CHAPTER
Sixteen
LANDFALL

Trenton followed Doris out of the lobby and into the darkened parking lot toward Miranda's car. Miranda had texted them both on the way there.

Of the people Jack worked with, he trusted Bill Winslow the most, but Bill was meek-mannered, and it would be unsettling to involve him at this point. Something had gone wrong when Trenton was brought in for his protection, so Jack was apprehensive about involving anyone from his department. And he agreed with Miranda that Doris and Trenton were more trustworthy and capable of handling the exchange than anyone else they could think of.

Doris had been the first to respond to the message, almost like she'd had her phone in hand. Even though she didn't want to involve Doris, Miranda was willing to gamble, based on what she'd seen of them in the woods yesterday, that they would be fine handling Aaron.

When Miranda saw Doris, a smile came to her face. She felt

an affection for Doris that reminded her of her love for her aunt.

Miranda suspected that to have such good intuition as Doris had about crime, beyond being trained as a nurse in Vietnam, she must have also received some form of military training. Or she was extremely well read and well informed, and Miranda hoped she herself would age so well. Doris was someone she wanted to stay in contact with after this case was over, along with Jack and possibly Trenton.

When Jack pulled the truck alongside the pair of honorary agents, Trenton hurried over to Jack's window and saw Aaron sitting in the back.

"He surrendered?" said Trenton.

"He's hoping to lead us to evidence that will save him," said Miranda. "And Jack and I have an errand to run, but we don't want to endanger both of you either."

"Did he talk about using my gun?"

"He testified on a video," said Jack. "Miranda has it."

Trenton refused to look at Aaron. He could feel his anger building and didn't want it to escalate.

"My impression is that word of the orchids is starting to circulate," said Trenton. "But there's a lot of misinformation and mining company talking points being repeated to counter it. I'm surprised by how many deniers are trying to say I'm still the killer and that the pictures of the orchids on social media are fake."

"If the deniers are out in force because the news of orchids upsets them, then maybe we're on to something by giving them the truth," said Miranda. "My impression is that Aaron is a pawn in this too, but he's a dangerous one, so don't give him any sympathy."

"And we hate involving you two," said Jack. "But you're the only two willing to stand with us right now."

"We feel honored to help," said Doris. She viewed it as a compliment to be handed such responsibility, and she accepted it was her civic obligation because Ethan Richards had chosen to target her. She'd accepted that role the day she'd had to leave her home.

She was looking at Miranda's leg, where her wound was concealed beneath her pants. She wanted to tell her to rest but knew they had to go forward with whatever pressed them to drop a murderer off into their custody. Miranda and Jack wouldn't have asked them unless they felt it was absolutely necessary to help them bring justice to David Willis and his family.

"I'm not comfortable with you two separating from us," said Doris. "The guys we met at my place a couple of days ago are still out there. You shouldn't be doing this alone."

"You should have told us you were leaving the hotel in the middle of the night," said Trenton.

"We're not going to involve you in all of our war games," said Miranda. "Only this last one."

"As long as people know there's copper here, the war games will never end," said Doris. "This won't be the last one."

"Then let's try showing any others who have ambitions like Ethan Richards they need to follow laws and have open discussions with the public," said Miranda. "Jack and I are going to Jeff Harvey's to search for a stash of documents, so don't mention it to anyone unless you don't hear from us in an hour. Don't deliver Aaron to the department until we've had time to check out the place. We don't know for sure who's involved in this, and we don't want Aaron talking to anyone until we're safe. We also don't want him gaining any sympathy by making it appear that he's helping us."

"We understand," said Doris.

"Once you drop him off, return to the hotel," said Miranda. "I don't think it's safe for either of you to be at your homes yet."

"My son may show up," said Jack. "I told him to stay in my room, so please check to see if he's there when you get back."

"Maybe we should all go," said Doris. "We work well as a team."

"You're already helping us way too much as it is," said Miranda. "I feel guilty for involving you as much as we have, but I don't see any other way."

She began gathering the weaponry from the front seat of Jack's truck and transferring it to her Camry. Among the weaponry, Doris noticed her rifle on the seat.

"If you won't take us with you, at least leave us the rifle just in case something happens," said Doris. "I always feel comfortable knowing I have my rifle."

Miranda remembered how Jack's use of the rifle at Doris's had saved them, so Miranda left the gun on the front seat of the truck for Doris and Trenton to take with them.

"You're doing enough by helping us to get out there before sunrise without alerting anyone," she said. "You and Trenton have a big enough responsibility than to come with us and get into a shootout. And if this backfires on us and we find something beyond our capabilities, then we're all meeting at the airport and going somewhere more pleasant."

Jack stepped out of his truck and gave Trenton the keys. After Miranda moved the guns to her car, she hugged Doris.

"Don't make any stops, and don't let Aaron out until you're at the station, no matter what," said Miranda. "Even if he has to pee, keep him in the backseat."

She handed Doris a pistol.

"David Willis and his family would be glad you're pursuing the money behind this even though you have the killer," said Doris.

"If the family was fully aware of what's happening, they'd be even happier to see community members getting involved when the police won't," said Miranda.

"I think we should leave now for the jail, but we'll take our time," said Trenton. "And we'll make sure he doesn't talk to anyone until we know you're safe. I like that better."

"Be alert," said Miranda. "This isn't Venezuela or South Sudan, but with thugs like Aaron arriving here to do whatever Ethan Richards asks, it isn't a far stretch either. We care about you both, so be safe."

Then she and Jack got into the Camry and drove away.

As Miranda drove, Jack texted Steve and Bill to let them know they had Aaron Pierce in custody and that Doris and Trenton would be bringing him in.

"I'm worried we're stepping far out on a limb," said Jack.

"I wouldn't have bothered them if I didn't think we needed the help," said Miranda. "My only hope is that when Steve sees

Trenton, he won't do something dumb like arrest him again, or worse."

Miranda grabbed his hand.

Jack could feel her tighten her grip before relaxing her fingers.

"You're a beautiful person, Miranda," said Jack. "And I don't want to see you get hurt again."

"That's why we're going to be as smart as we can about this," Miranda replied.

"I'm wondering if you weren't right."

"About what?"

"I'm inclined to think because of the lack of support and everything we've already been through, maybe we should let them win this time."

"I thought that way earlier, but I've never been given a chance like this, where everything that can bring justice to these people is located in one tidy package. And we're a strong team together. I wouldn't think about doing this if you weren't with me."

"We need a game plan then because Jeff's place isn't far."

"The plan is simple. We park down the street, and I move for the shed. When we're finished, we go back to taking care of ourselves—relaxing, avoiding getting caught up in any more messes like these. But until then, we get there, and I'm in and out in under two minutes. You cover me like you've been doing. There's no point in changing a good thing. And maybe I'm being a martyr, but I need to make this one last effort."

"I'm with you, Miranda. You don't have to justify your actions to me."

Miranda explained that in light of the lack of support from their departments, the reality was that no matter what they found in Jeff's garden shed, even if there was anything incriminating, Ethan Richards' involvement in conspiring to commit murder might go unpunished this time.

"What I'm really hoping for is to bring any documents to light so the public can view them, which will require a public platform to display them. The community of Clearwater and the residents of Wisconsin will have to be the ones to decide if they're going to stand for people like Ethan Richards controlling their futures."

"What about a warrant?"

"We don't need one if we suspect evidence could be destroyed. Plus, you and I don't have the power or the backing to bring it to court anyway. It's so the people can finally see the truth."

"What if the shed is locked?" said Jack.

"I have bolt cutters in the trunk under the weapons. I wish we would have asked Aaron more questions, but we're up against time because I was hoping to make use of the darkness," said Miranda. "We're always up against time."

Then she touched his hand.

"I don't let many people in my life, so be careful," she said. "I don't want to be made an example in the FBI training manual for being that FBI agent who was dumb for trusting someone like Aaron Pierce. But I don't want to miss the one real chance to bring down Ethan Richards either."

They parked at a boat landing down the street from Jeff's house so that no one would be suspicious of car doors closing. Several fishermen were launching boats through the fog at the boat ramp, but the fishermen were too concerned with preparing the boats and getting on the water for the early morning bite. Miranda handed Jack several extra magazine clips, grabbed the bolt cutters from the trunk, then quietly closed the compartment.

As they walked up the street past several quaint lake houses, Miranda questioned if Jeff's house was as nice as those they passed. Remembering back to the condition of *The Chronicle*, she asked Jack where Jeff had gotten the money to afford lakefront property. Jack told her he'd inherited the home from his grandparents.

A jogger passed them on the winding street lined with spacious lake houses on the left and a towering cliff on the right, but the man seemed too plugged into the music to notice Jack wearing his police jacket and the woman beside him carrying bright red bolt cutters.

When they reached Jeff's house, tucked into one of the coves in a bay on the big lake, there was a "For Sale" sign out front. No lights were on. No vehicle was in sight, but there was a garage, so they had to assume and play it as though Jeff was most likely at home sleeping.

The ten feet wide by twelve feet long white garden shed at the far back corner of the yard still sported wooden siding, which looked like it had roughly ten coats of latex paint built up on it, indicating it had been built around the fifties or sixties. It was nestled up against the lake.

"He's listing his house, getting out before everyone else understands the lake is about to disappear," Miranda whispered.

"It's odd," said Jack.

"What is?"

"Ten years ago, Jeff swore he'd never sell that house."

"Maybe they're pressuring him to go along?"

"Maybe, but it isn't like him to ditch the community."

They stopped along the street at the far edge of the back of the house. Miranda scanned the property for cameras. She didn't see any trail cameras. And even if she had, she wasn't worried about the legality of using the evidence for a court case and having it thrown out due to an illegal search. She only wanted the public to know about the evidence and judge it for themselves. But she was worried about security cameras that could alert people like Ethan Richards or Jeff Harvey to their presence. She didn't see any of those either. And it was morning, just before full daylight, so the likelihood of anyone watching backyard monitors for intruders seemed unlikely.

She moved swiftly toward the shed. Jack followed and took up watch behind a big weeping willow tree at the corner of the yard, near the road. The willow tree fronds moved in the gentle morning air, and the road was quiet. Jack, wearing his bulletproof vest under his police jacket, had his fingertips on the gun in case he needed to protect Miranda. He watched her, leaving footprints in the heavy dew, sprint across the green manicured lawn and over to the shed.

The wooden door of the shed was unlocked. Miranda didn't think it was too unusual because the contents of such a small space weren't worth the hassle of locking. She placed her bolt cutters on the grass and slipped inside with ease. She closed the door behind herself.

Jack sighed. As he waited for Miranda to emerge, the passing of time felt like a year to him. He looked back on the past couple of days. It was far too soon for him to say that he loved her, but he was getting to the age where he had been questioning if he'd ever love anyone again. Miranda made him feel alive again, like he hadn't felt in years. *It's like I've been given a second chance at life,* he thought.

Miranda had been inside for only a minute when Jack saw a black SUV pull into Jeff's driveway at the front of the house. Before it turned into the driveway, he could see the broken mirror he'd shot two days before, and he recognized, even from a distance, the two men he fired upon sitting in the front.

"The world was balanced in our favor for a moment," said Jack.

From behind the willow tree, he cupped his hands around his mouth. Before the SUV came to a complete stop, he shouted toward the garden shed, "Miranda!" But Miranda was still in the shed, seventy yards away. As soon as the men stepped out of the cab, he couldn't shout any longer.

In a millisecond, Jack's mind tried to process why they might be there. His first reaction was rage that Aaron had set them up. He wanted to open fire and run at the men before they knew what had hit them. But then he wondered if Doris and Trenton had been ambushed back at the hotel or on their way to the police station and tortured into giving up their position. The thought of his and Miranda's decision to hand Aaron over to their care made him feel sick. It was easier to think that the men's arrival was coincidental. Maybe if he sat tight and gave them time, they'd go in the house. Aaron's story, which corroborated Miranda's theory, was that Jeff was involved in accepting payment for spreading fake stories about the killing, so it was logical these men could be stopping by the lake house to pay him a visit.

Before he could decide what to do, three more men got out of the SUV, which had tinted windows. The group gathered in the driveway. Guns weren't drawn, but Jack suspected they were concealed under their jackets. Derrick, whom Jack had fired upon at Doris's house, began signaling for the men to spread out and to move toward the back of the house toward the garden shed. That's when the men drew their guns.

"At least I got to see my son one last time and make amends," Jack said to himself as he clicked the safety off of his pistol. "I knew this would be an ambitious pursuit, but we almost made it. I'll look after you, Miranda."

In the darkness of the windowless garden shed, Miranda turned the flashlight feature of her phone on to illuminate her cramped surroundings. She scanned for anything obvious among the yard equipment—a leaf blower, lawnmower, hedge trimmer, pruning shears—but she saw nothing that indicated the shed might contain valuable information about a mining company's corrupt intent. There was nothing beyond the ordinary gardening and yard tools.

"Aaron Pierce," Miranda whispered, "I'll grind your bones to dust."

She was about to emerge from the darkness when she took one last look around. She noticed a Folgers can high up on a shelf with its yellow lid. It was one of the old cans with a picture of a clipper ship on it. *What lake house didn't have an old Folgers can full of nuts and bolts and cotter pins*, she thought. But it was its inconspicuous nature that had her reaching for it.

At first glance, the can contained papers, envelopes, a voice recorder, and SD cards—anything but the fasteners and bolts needed to patch up a lawn mower or weed whacker.

Her hand was on the door handle when she heard the first gunshots.

She nearly dropped the can because she'd been so convinced that by finding evidence, they were in the clear and that Aaron hadn't lied to her.

Another shot came from behind her and to her left. That one was Jack, she thought.

In an instant, the decaying feeling of betrayal Miranda had been so careful to avoid spread through every nerve of her body.

She thought of Jack and felt the heaviness of her body dragging her down toward the floor. She felt the shame of being so stupid as to trust Aaron, a killer, and her hope that told her to take a chance and trust him.

Even though the coffee can contained a voice recorder, SD cards, official-looking papers with the State of Wisconsin emblems on them, and a folded map with yellow highlighting outlined properties extending for miles, Miranda thought they'd been set up. Her wish to trust that there was still a hint of goodness in the world would be responsible for her and Jack's demise.

And if there could never be any trust placed upon the institutions to help them or hold people like Aaron or Ethan Richards accountable, what had been the point of endangering her life by holding back from killing them? Why even try bringing in people like these to be prosecuted before the justice system? When it came to money, justice was rarely served and never deterred anyone from taking what they wanted anyway. They only prosecuted people like her, Jack, Trenton, or Doris. She knew it was moments like this that her aunt Rita and the detective on the beach had cautioned her about years ago.

"Why does doing the right thing always come with such a price?" Miranda wondered aloud. "You people who leave others hanging because of fear and selfishness need to disappear from the planet, but you won't."

When she burst from the shed, her gun was drawn, and she was trying to gain her bearing as she scanned the lawn for targets. Miranda tucked the Folgers can protectively between her left hand and arm like a wide receiver searching for the end zone after catching the ball. She decided that running to Jack would be too far of a distance with all of the gunfire. And when she saw no obvious targets standing in the open, she ran around to the back of the shed instead.

She peeked around the other side toward the house and saw someone sprawled out on the lawn. The man was face down, wasn't moving, and appeared to be dead. Looking over her left shoulder toward the willow tree, she saw Jack frantically motioning for her to come toward him. Miranda was overjoyed he was alive. Her second thought was that if she could make it to the willow tree without dying, how would they ever hold off several gunmen when they couldn't expect anyone to come and help them? They'd be trapped worse than they were now.

She tried remembering the number of gunshots she'd heard and the directions they'd come from to determine how many men there were. Three or four men, she guessed. Jack continued waving frantically to convince her to run toward him, suggesting there were others she had to worry about. But instead of running into the open yard she would have to cross to get to him, Miranda looked behind her, searching for another way out of the ambush. She saw fifty yards behind her, through some brush, saplings, and honeysuckle bushes, a small inlet connected to the main lake with a fishing boat anchored to a dock. The motor on the boat wasn't big, but it had a pull rope, which meant no key was required to start it. She motioned for Jack to follow her, then she took off running for the boat.

When Jack saw her run, he now understood he was going to have to be the one to run across the open lawn to get to her. He fired again at one of the men he had already wounded, and then, when he lowered his gun to run, he noticed blood dripping from the fingertips of his left hand. As the man kept coming toward him, Jack stepped out from the cover of the willow tree and fired again. The man he'd wounded dropped.

Jack sprinted in Miranda's direction toward the boat.

Derrick and the two remaining men opened fire on Jack, who found safety behind the shed. They had seen Miranda dart from the shed to find shelter behind it, but they hadn't had time to shoot at her because their focus and aim had been on Jack. They hadn't seen her or Jack dash for the boat because the shed blocked their view.

The men converged on the shed. With his gun drawn, Derrick kicked open the door to ensure no one else was inside. The other two crept around to the backside. Absent from the group was the driver they'd met at Doris's. Had Jack had the time to look, he would have realized the driver was the first man he'd shot. He was lying dead on the lawn.

When Jack leapt into the boat, Miranda already had the motor running. She opened the throttle on the twenty-five horsepower Johnson outboard motor. The engine coughed and smoked, but then its synchronized machinery caught and worked in unison to propel the boat onto the main lake. Miranda pushed the tiller handle to the left to turn the boat to the right in order to use the other lake houses and contour of the lake to shield them from more gunfire. When she'd hit the throttle, Jack fell backward into the bottom of the boat. They were safe for the moment.

When Miranda saw blood dripping from Jack's fingertips, which judging by the steady drip and stream down his hand, originated somewhere higher up on his arm, she let go of the throttle and leapt forward, causing the boat to nearly stop dead in the water. She lurched forward, allowing the boat to drift aimlessly as she tried to help him to remove his jacket. She was desperate to see the extent of the injury.

"We aren't far enough away to examine anything yet," said Jack, pushing her toward the tiller motor. "We have to keep going."

"How bad is it?" Miranda asked.

"It's the outside of my arm. Just outside the reach of my bulletproof vest."

"Are you sure it's your arm? Did it shatter bone?"

"Yes, I'm sure it's my arm, and no, it didn't go through bone, or maybe it did, and I'm in shock. But now isn't the time to determine that."

Miranda moved back to the bench seat near the tiller motor, wrapped her hand around the throttle, twisted it to the right, and brought the engine to maximum speed again.

She didn't think Jack was in shock, although she could see his awareness of how close he had been to being killed. The first time it happened to her, she experienced a feeling of insignificance and helplessness she would never forget.

"They'll be following us along the shoreline, or they'll find a boat to follow us," said Miranda.

"Being on the water in a boat is better than where we were, but it still isn't good. How much gas is in the can?"

Having rested the coffee can on the bench seat beside her, Miranda lifted the red metal tank with the black hose feeding the boat engine.

"It feels like a gallon, maybe two."

They looked along the shoreline for places to hide and to further evaluate the extent of Jack's bullet wound, but there was nothing but homes. They didn't want to endanger anyone in the community by bringing the war to them. And they didn't know who they could trust, and they refused to hide in someone's house and be trapped in door-to-door searches. They couldn't see any other boats to steal that would be any faster. For now, they'd keep going because they were safe together. There was temporary comfort in that.

Jack finally noticed the Folgers coffee can nestled beside her.

"Running low on caffeine?" he said, gritting his teeth.

"It's what we came for. It's all there."

"Then it's just like Aaron said."

"If everything inside of it isn't fake, we're probably in serious trouble, but you know that already."

"What happened back there?" asked Jack.

"I don't know. I don't want to think about it," said Miranda. "We did what we thought was right, so don't second guess involving Trenton and Doris or the fact that you're bleeding. I can't think about any of it right now. I want to get somewhere safe."

As Jack pressed against his wound to slow the bleeding, he let the idea of betrayal by Aaron (or whatever could have possibly gone wrong) fade away. He tried thinking of what they would need to get back to land and to the safety of the hotel. A car, a friend? A safe place to be picked up before they were tracked down and killed? All he could think of was Doris, Trenton, and his son.

And he and Miranda would need somewhere to dock besides a public boat landing where more goons would most likely be waiting for them. At least they had to assume they were being chased. They didn't consider calling Jack's or Miranda's departments for help. It wasn't even a possibility at this point. He felt helpless, and it was then that he fully appreciated Miranda because she had known all along how alone they were, yet she had stayed with him from the beginning.

Considering the limited amount of gas, the only place Jack could think of where someone could safely pick them up was Baker's Bay, a secluded part of the lake that no longer had a boat landing. There was barely even a road there anymore, but all the locals, especially Doris's generation, knew where it was. From what Jack had heard, there used to be a bar and a restaurant there that had been torn down years ago when the state acquired the land for the state park. But it was far across the other side of the lake.

"There's a bay, more of a cove that only the locals know about," said Jack.

"Where?"

"There," said Jack. He let go of his wounded shoulder and pointed toward the far end of the lake with his right hand.

"But if we run out of gas before we get there," he said, "we'll be in more trouble than we're already in."

"If we have to get in the water and abandon the boat and the evidence, then so be it. I'll do what I can to make sure you're safe, Jack. It's my fault you're here."

"I don't want your apology. You're not the one who shot me. They're the reason we're in this mess, not you."

Miranda felt some relief in knowing he wasn't angry with her. She veered the boat toward where Jack had pointed.

Of the few people he knew he could rely on, Jack decided to call Doris even though he was worried something had happened to her and Trenton and that she wouldn't answer. He took out his phone. His blood smeared the screen as he searched for her in his contacts. The wet droplets were affecting the functionality of his call button, but he got it to work.

When Doris answered, he forgot about the blood and the pain in his shoulder.

"Doris!" he shouted. "Are you there?"

He had to speak loudly so she could hear him over the racing outboard motor. He wondered if he should have called his son instead, but he would have been too emotional to relay instructions. And this wasn't a goodbye type of phone call. He was ecstatic to hear Doris's voice, not just because she was a lifeline but because she was alive, which maybe meant they hadn't been ambushed. Maybe part of their plan had worked.

"Are you guys okay?" he asked. But Jack didn't think he should wait for an answer in case he lost service.

"Something went wrong. Miranda and I need you to pick us up at Baker's Bay," he said. "Do you know where it is?"

Jack couldn't hear for certain, but he thought Doris said, "Yes."

"Baker's Bay. There used to be a bar there years ago. We're coming by boat. Miranda's okay. I'm hit in the shoulder, but we got what we came for. It was there in the shed like it was supposed to be."

Jack struggled to hear her response the second time, but he was convinced he heard her say that she knew where Baker's Bay was and that she'd be there.

"How did the drop with Aaron go?" he asked.
He heard Doris say something about Trenton and Aaron, but then she cut out.

"Say it again!" he shouted into the phone.

He waited for Doris to say something, but nothing came through.

The signal was lost.

He hit redial on the bloodied screen, but they were in a dead spot. The call wouldn't go through.

"As far as I could tell, Doris knows where it is and is meeting us there," said Jack. "We might make it out of this. At the very least, she sounded okay and knows where we are."

"That's somewhat of a relief because if anything had happened to her, I don't know what I'd do."

They scanned the water and saw no other boats coming their way. Because the lake was so vast, they also didn't see any fishermen with bigger, faster boats who might be able to help them. Jack took the time to reload his pistol. Then nothing more could be done, so he assessed the damage to his arm. He strained to remove his rain jacket and saw the wound. It was just like he'd said. The bullet had passed through the outer part of his shoulder. Somehow it had missed bone and his rotator cuff. But it was still bleeding badly.

"Check in the bow for a first aid kit," said Miranda.

Jack searched a compartment toward the front. He knew there was a good chance of finding a kit because fishermen often carried them on the big lake. A faded white first aid kit with surface rust was tucked under some lifejackets in the rectangular aluminum compartment. Inside the kit were bandages and tape. The bandages were probably from the seventies or eighties, but they were still in their original packages and seemed sterile. Even if they weren't, it didn't matter under the circumstances. Jack used them to apply pressure and slow the bleeding. He held the bandages against his damaged shoulder as they rode across the lake.

Jack looked at the gas can as if he were trying to will it to contain enough fuel to make it. He was hoping he wouldn't hear the motor slow and then sputter to an abrupt stop. To keep Miranda on course and maximize fuel consumption, he often pointed out the way to keep her on course.

They were more than halfway across the lake when Jack saw a boat three-quarters of a mile behind them on the same path as they were.

"We don't need that," he said. "Where the hell did they get a boat so fast?"

With her right hand wrenching on the throttle of the tiller handle, trying to make the boat go faster, Miranda looked over her right shoulder. She saw it was a larger boat with more speed than theirs. Looking ahead to where they had yet to travel, the boat would overtake them before they reached Baker's Bay.

"I didn't see a boat at Jeff's. They must have made a call to someone who's on the water," said Miranda. "Why is it that the bad guys always get whatever they need?"

"Because it makes them feel like they have the upper hand."

"They do have the upper hand. They've had it this whole time."

"If that were true, we'd have been dead a long time ago."

They looked for a piece of land jutting out into the water close enough to run the boat aground and make a run for it. It didn't have to be near Baker's Bay, but nothing was close.

"Now is probably a good time to tell you that you're good for me, Jack," said Miranda. "This whole time, you haven't made me feel ashamed of who I am or for anything I've done."

"That's great, but we aren't finished yet. We have to keep fighting. You're the one who's made me realize we can't ever back down from these people."

Jack strained to see the boat's occupants, but the only one he was sure about was Derrick, the man who'd threatened them at the farmhouse. He recognized him by his posture and from shooting at him again at Jeff's. There were four others, but he couldn't tell who they were, yet there was no question they were on a direct path to catch up with them.

"I know one of them is your goon from Doris's," said Jack. "I couldn't get a clean shot at him at Jeff's. I don't know about the others, but there are five of them."

"With your shooting, we might stand a chance. We can still shoot at them to keep them at a distance. And reception might not be good enough to call Doris again, but see if you can text her. Tell her we need someone to get that boat away from us."

Jack wasted no time getting his bloodied phone out, but texting was difficult as a breeze came across the water, making gentle rollers that made the ride bumpy. Once Jack finally typed the message, he had to keep hitting the red exclamation point button to resend the message several times. Eventually, the "failed to send" message stopped popping up, so it appeared to go through to Doris.

"We should have handed over Aaron ourselves and been done with this case," said Miranda.

"We did what was right," said Jack. "Don't ever question that."

The motor was too loud to hear the gunshots, but bullets began to hit the water alongside them as though someone had dropped a stick of dynamite next to the boat, sending a splash of water four feet in the air.

"We're in rifle range," said Jack.

"But they're contending with the waves. Start shooting back."

The location where Doris was supposed to meet them was still a quarter of a mile away.

She'll have to hurry, Jack thought.

He judged the boat behind them to be one hundred fifty yards away and closing. The only thing saving them from taking a direct hit was the choppiness of the waves, and the men behind them couldn't keep their sights fixed on them. Jack could easily see the men in the boat behind them aiming at them, and it was a sense of helplessness he'd never before experienced. There was nowhere in the open bow of their boat to go for safety or shelter. The aluminum sides were too thin to stop a bullet, so it wasn't like they could lie at the bottom or even duck down for protection.

Even though Jack figured the boat was still too far away for him to do any damage with a pistol, he listened to Miranda and fired a couple of quick shots. He was surprised it caused them to veer from their course. It gave him a glimmer of hope. He decided to aim at the driver.

He brought the pistol sights level with his eyes, but he wasn't steady enough. The waves made the boat a poor shooting platform. It pained him to think about raising his left arm, but he knew he had to do it. He gritted his teeth when he raised his bloodied left hand to help steady the gun. With both eyes opened, he aimed a foot high. But he couldn't focus at such a distance with both eyes open, so he shut his left eye and squeezed it tight. He brought the gun closer to his face to narrow the space between the metal sights. He forgot about the throbbing in his arm. He took a breath and held it while he let his body and muscles absorb the shock of the waves so he could remain steady. To Jack's astonishment, the man he'd put the sights on was flung backward a second after he fired. It was as though a force as heavy as a refrigerator had hit him.

"I don't know how, but I hit the driver!"

"I hope it was Ethan Richards. That would be justice. And if we survive this, I'm going to rethink government agency work. Following the rules is to our disadvantage when dealing with criminals like these."

Shooting the driver was enough to put the boat off course. It also put the boat out of range for Jack's pistol to reach them. But the moment was fleeting. Someone else shoved the driver's body onto the floor and got behind the wheel. In no time, the boat was in their wake, threatening them again.

"If I jump out, you might make it," said Jack.

"Don't be stupid."

"Then what do you suggest?"

"I'm thinking."

Miranda attempted to organize her scattered thoughts.

"A SWAT team and helicopters would be nice," said Jack.

"Yes, it would. If only we knew someone at the FBI with the right connections."

Jack fired at the men again, but both boats were now moving in a zigzag formation, trying to avoid taking direct hits from the gunfire. Jack was only firing randomly now, trying to keep them at bay.

Jack emptied the clip to the pistol and slammed in another.

Miranda lifted the gas can. She guessed that it weighed about five pounds, including the metal container. They had less than half a gallon.

"We're going to be just short of land," said Miranda.

"We're going to have to surrender," said Jack. "We're nearly out of ammo."

"These aren't the types to surrender to."

"That's too bad," Jack said. "Because as horrible as this case has been, ever since you came to Clearwater, my life has started making sense."

He fired several more rounds until the clip was empty. He had only one full clip, giving him fifteen more rounds. With Miranda's pistol, they had another fifteen. But with rifles in the other boat, they were completely out-gunned.

The motor coughed. Miranda looked back to see how far the other boat was. As long as Jack fired at them, the boat held back about one hundred fifty yards, just beyond the range that any of them could shoot on the water with repetitive accuracy.

"If you can hold them off and make it to shore, we stand a chance. How quickly can Doris get here from town?"

"Maybe ten minutes from when I called," said Jack. "But she'd have to be moving."

"I pushed it too far, Jack. I'm sorry."

"It's not you. It's them. And no matter what happens, I feel good that we never made any compromises."

When they were three hundred yards from shore at Baker's Bay, the motor coughed some more and sputtered. And then it surged as it sucked in oxygen and the last gulp of the fuel. Then it died. As the boat drifted toward shore, which was still far off, Jack kept firing his gun until the clip was empty.

Before the boat came to a complete stop, Miranda tucked the Folgers can under the seat, removed her jacket, and frantically shoved her pistol in her pants to conceal it. Then she leapt into the cold water.

Jack, out of bullets and thinking that Miranda was doing the right thing by trying to save herself, hung his head and dropped his gun to the bottom of the boat.

Bullets started hitting the water all around them. The men in the other boat were toying with them now. They saw that Jack had thrown down his weapon.

Standing alongside Derrick, who was driving the boat, was Ethan Richards. Miranda recognized him as she stopped swimming away from them and started treading water. She was hoping they'd think she was unarmed and had ditched Jack. She continued to tread water and looked up at the men as the boat circled them. It was the first good look they had of Ethan Richards. Miranda thought he looked as creepy in person as he had in the photo she'd seen of him on the internet.

"Ethan Richards," shouted Miranda. "FBI. I know we've

done our job when people like you show up."

"Worthless public servants. You both took something from Jeff Harvey's house," said Ethan gazing down at Miranda. "It belongs to us."

He didn't seem interested in Jack as two other men kept their guns on him.

Derrick remained sitting in the driver's seat, maneuvering the boat closer. He wore the same shitty, arrogant smirk Miranda had seen at the farmhouse.

"Anything we have belongs to the people of Clearwater," said Miranda. "And you're under arrest for the first-degree murder of David Willis."

Ethan and the others smirked.

"How are you planning on arresting us?" Ethan asked.

"I'm still working on it," said Miranda, frantically treading water and searching for other boaters.

"I'm a job creator, so you have an odd moral compass to think I've done anything wrong that will ever land me in jail. The FBI and the community of Clearwater need to do a better job screening their employees."

"The employees are fine. It's arrogant management like you that's the problem," said Miranda.

Jack had been admiring his handiwork as he looked at the dead driver, now splayed on the floor. His bullet had hit the man in the throat and had caught part of his chin. He was still recognizable.

"That's Senator McLeary," said Jack. "I always knew there was something shady about him."

"He was a good friend and political ally who will be difficult to replace," said Ethan. "Send the detective to the bottom of the lake so he can join Jeff Harvey."

Immediately after Ethan said it, one of the men shot Jack in the chest with a rifle. It hit him with such force it knocked him backward out of the boat. Although he was wearing his bullet-proof vest, the concussion of the bullet compressed his ribcage against his lungs, forcing the air out to such an extent that while underwater, he gasped for air. He struggled with his arms and kicked with his legs to get to the surface, but the weight of his clothing, including his bulletproof vest and injured arm, dragged him toward the bottom.

"Jack!" Miranda screamed, spinning in the water toward Jack in time to see him go under. She tried to pull out the gun she'd tucked in her pants, but just as she pulled the gun up and before she could shoot, Derrick threw a rope around her neck and began dragging her toward them.

Miranda lost the gun as she fought and gasped and clawed at the rope. She struggled to breathe as Derrick hoisted her up, partway out of the water. Her head banged against the hard fiberglass side of the boat.

"Find whatever they took," said Ethan Richards.

One of the men leapt into the small fishing boat. He immediately produced the coffee can.

"I've dealt with resistance all my life," Ethan said to Miranda. "But I've never seen anyone become so attached to landscapes and flowers and third-class citizens. And that biologist was the same. If he'd done his job and accepted the money, then all of you would be alive. But some of you still haven't learned your place in this new age of business and technology. Bring her in the boat so we can teach her to respect the people who drive this world economy."

Miranda tried to speak but didn't have the breath with the rope tight around her throat.

Derrick reached for her hair to drag her into the boat, but before he even put a hand on her, a bullet ripped through the center of his forehead. The rope released from his grip, and Miranda slipped back into the water. Derrick's knees buckled, and his body collapsed in a heap to the bottom of the boat.

Realizing she'd been released from the noose, Miranda frantically clawed the rope away from her neck, came up to the surface, and gasped for air until her lungs were full. Then she dove down again to try and retrieve Jack.

The two men in the boat left holding guns were dazed to

see the two corpses lying in pools of blood at their feet.

Ethan Richards ducked and scanned the shoreline as he tried to make sense of who was shooting at them.

"It came from shore over there!" he shouted.

As the other two men realized where the gunshot had come from, they began firing toward the distant shoreline, but only for a second. A bullet went through each of their heads—first one, then the other a second apart. The only one alive now in the boat was Ethan Richards.

"You're firing on an unarmed man who has government connections! You're all going to regret this!"

Keeping his head out of sight, he stepped over the bodies and made his way over to the driver's seat. The boat was still idling, so he put the drive in gear, pushed the throttle wide open, and spun the steering wheel back in the direction they'd come. He'd gone a hundred yards before he felt safe enough to lift his head to look around. He figured he was out of the range of gunfire. When he lifted his chin to get a better look at the direction of his course, the back of his head exploded. He slumped against the steering wheel, causing it to turn right. The boat began spinning in wide circles.

When Miranda surfaced with Jack, he was limp. She struggled with the waves to tread water while supporting Jack and breathing into his mouth. Jack remained lifeless. She didn't even notice that the boat had left.

"Jack!" Miranda screamed. She took a deep breath and gave him more air. She swam toward the rocky shoreline, dragging Jack with her, breathing into his mouth between every third stroke.

When they got to shore, Miranda unzipped Jack's vest, rolled him on his side, and pounded on his back to get the water out. Then she gave him more air and pounded on his chest again. She did it to the point of exhaustion. She put her head in her hands and started sobbing.

Jack coughed and gasped for air. He rolled to the side, vomited, and gasped some more. Before he even had oxygen in his lungs, Miranda hugged him and pulled him close.

"I thought we were both dead," cried Miranda.

Jack pushed her to the side so he could breathe. He coughed and gagged.

"What happened?" said Jack.

"Someone shot them. I'm not sure who."

Miranda kissed him, and then she helped him move from his back to a sitting position. It was then that she noticed Doris climbing down from the boulders and coming toward them carrying her rifle.

Doris navigated through the rocks to the shoreline, where Jack was still recovering. When she got close, she saw that Jack was pale as he struggled to catch his breath.

"Is he okay?" she asked.

"I think so. His arm will need fixing. He probably has a broken rib, but he wore his vest. He was shot at such close range that I thought the bullet would penetrate, but it didn't."

"What happened?" said Jack.

"In their board meetings, they miscalculated the cost of stealing this area from the people," said Doris. "And they underestimated the talent of an old woman."

"Where's Trenton, Doris?" asked Miranda.

"Don't either of you feel guilty about this," said Doris, "but I drove him to the hospital. He's undergoing surgery for a gunshot wound to his chest. He was conscious. I think he has a collapsed lung."

"They ambushed you?"

"Right after you left, I went back to the hotel room because I forgot my phone. When I came out, Trenton was slumped over in the seat, and Aaron was gone. I tried calling Miranda to warn you they'd be headed your way if Aaron talked, but I didn't get through."

Miranda stood and gazed out at the lake as she worried about Trenton. She watched the speedboat going in circles.

She could see several Department of Natural Resources and police boats with flashing red and blue strobes beating across the water, moving toward the speedboat and coming directly at them. When the boats reached her, she would make sure the coffee can was retrieved.

"Doris, we should get Jack to a hospital and check on Trenton," said Miranda.

Miranda wrapped her arms around Doris and squeezed her tight.

"I'm so sorry you had to do everything you've done," said Miranda. "We owe you everything."

"This wasn't the first time I've had to kill. As I told you earlier, I know what surviving a war requires," said Doris.

"This wasn't the ending I had in mind, but as long as Trenton survives, it worked."

Miranda hugged her one last time.

CHAPTER
Seventeen
WHITE SANDS

Miranda lay on a towel on the beach in a pink bikini. Behind her was the Ritz Carlton hotel. The white sand stretched for miles. She had a surfboard on the sand in front of her. Jack, shirtless, wearing tan shorts, his arm in a sling, and a bruise on his chest, strolled up to her and handed her a margarita.

"Isn't it too early for you to be drinking?" said Miranda.

"Not while I'm on vacation, and I could get used to this life," said Jack. "I don't know if I want to go back."

"You have a week to think about it."

"I was thinking this morning that the whole thing still feels unresolved. I would rather have seen Ethan Richards being dragged through trial and sentenced. It would have been more satisfying."

"We've talked about this. Ethan Richards chose to end it the way he did because he would never give us the satisfaction of putting him in jail. He felt he was too good for the people of

Clearwater to ever be held accountable."

"It's unfortunate to reach a point where you believe you're above the law and everyone else. It seems to lead to so much ruin."

"And now detectives like us have come under fire for not bending the rules for them, and I don't know if I'll get used to the change. So I thought of something else we can do that doesn't involve so much agony."

"What's that?"

"Travel writing."

"You said writing doesn't reach the people who need reaching."

"It doesn't, but maybe it's someone else's turn to do what they think is best to help save the next Clearwater."

Jack sat on the towel on the sand next to her.

"I don't agree with that. If we'd have relied on others, I'm not sure where Clearwater would be. And we did get a "thank you" from a South American president," said Jack.

"True. So maybe we are in the right line of work. Maybe just not in the right departments," said Miranda. "Sniping might align more with our talents, especially with you and Doris. And I was thinking the next time we travel, we need to make sure Doris and Trenton can make it."

"So there will be a next time?"

"Of course. You're not leaving my side for a long time."

"I'll try to keep up with you, but you have to remember I'm older."

"But not slower."

Jack looked out at the ocean.

"I bet Doris would love Aruba," said Jack. "She could paint some beautiful landscapes."

"She texted before you got out here," Miranda said. "She's painting orchids, and she's going to send pictures so we can pick out which ones we want."

"After you left the room, I called Trenton to check on what's happening back home. He's still healing. He's spearheading a campaign to make people aware of everything Clearwater has to offer, not just copper. The people at Global Econ are talking. It sounds like they're willing to re-examine their practices. And apparently, Steve apologized to Trenton, but not to me."

"I know they found Jeff's body in the lake, but what about Aaron's?"

"No word yet, but if he doesn't turn up, I won't lose sleep over him. He told them exactly where we were going, but thankfully, we had Doris. And we won because of you, and that's what I want to focus on, but you also couldn't have done it without me."

"I know, Jack. You did a lot of the shooting."

"That's not it. The biggest part was that I was smart enough to call you."

He stood, took off his sling, grabbed the surfboard, and headed for the water.

"What are you doing?" asked Miranda. "You said you don't know how to surf."

"Not yet, but I can learn from you. I need to think of something I can teach you."

Miranda got up from the sand and put down her drink.

The two of them walked toward the warm ocean water.

"A lot of good things came from being sent to Clearwater," said Miranda. "I found you, and I don't hate detective work as long as we're together. And Clearwater seems to have a sense of balance to its community again."

Jack carried the surfboard under his right arm toward the crashing waves, and before he even hit the water, he knew he'd fallen for her.

ACKNOWLEDGEMENTS

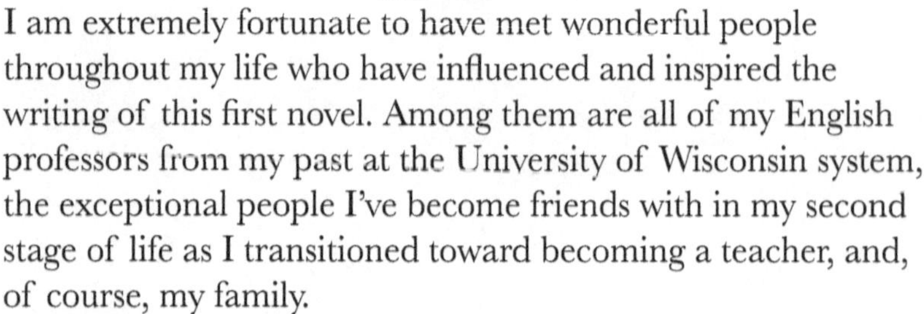

I am extremely fortunate to have met wonderful people throughout my life who have influenced and inspired the writing of this first novel. Among them are all of my English professors from my past at the University of Wisconsin system, the exceptional people I've become friends with in my second stage of life as I transitioned toward becoming a teacher, and, of course, my family.

Special thanks go to Tracy Reynolds for editing the rough draft, coming up with a great title, and being such a fabulous friend and colleague. Thank you, Chuck Stingley, for doing an initial read-through of the story and being that guy who dove into the water so many years ago to save his friend's fishing trip. Thank you, Shannon Booth, for your unique insight into story development and bringing cadence and rhythm to the dialogue and description. Thank you, Officer Summer Karll, for volunteering your spare time to make sure the storyline followed law enforcement protocol. Thank you, Rachel Anderson, for your work on the interior design. Thank you, Webb Middle School colleagues, for being the incredible friends and support group you are. And thank you, Dana Westedt, for the conversations and confidence you've given me in my pursuit of writing.

Most of all, I thank my wife, Cindi, for supporting me and helping me become the individual I am today. The completion of this book signifies a milestone in my life, which I have been able to reach only because she has stood by my side. Thank you, beautiful!

ABOUT THE AUTHOR

I am an English teacher living in a rural southwestern Wisconsin community. My wife and I are both teachers and own a small vineyard. When I'm not teaching eighth graders, writing stories, or working in the vineyard, I'm golfing or fishing with my best friends.